All day long, Hayden had been walking on a tightrope. That rope was way too close to snapping.

A man had come after Jill. He'd shot at her...

"You aren't staying here alone tonight."

Her eyes widened. "Uh, excuse me?"

"That intruder—"

"I think I did a pretty good job of defending mysel

She didn't get it. "Do you want me to stay sane?"

Her brow furrowed. "That would probably be a good plan."

He thought so, too. Hayden nodded. "Then, you're staying with me tonight. I'll have a deputy keep watch on your place."

She crossed her arms over her chest. "Did you jus tell me I was staying at your place?"

"I did." He inclined his head toward her.

"I'm not afraid, Hayden. If he comes back, I'll be ready for him. I'll be—"

"I know you're not scared." He got that. What she didn't get... "I am."

She laughed. "Right, the big, bad navy SEAL is afraid. You're—"

"Absolutely terrified that something will happen to you."

ABDUCTION

—

New York Times Bestselling Author
CYNTHIA EDEN

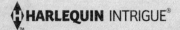 HARLEQUIN INTRIGUE®

I want to dedicate this book to Elaine—
the absolute best mother-in-law that a girl could ever have!
Elaine, thank you so much for your support over the years.
This Intrigue is for you.

ISBN-13: 978-0-373-75663-6

Recycling programs
for this product may
not exist in your area.

Abduction

Copyright © 2017 by Cindy Roussos

Printed in U.S.A.

www.Harlequin.com

Cynthia Eden is a *New York Times* and *USA TODAY* bestselling author. She writes dark tales of romantic suspense and paranormal romance. Her books have received starred reviews from *Publishers Weekly*, and one was named a 2013 RITA® finalist for best romantic suspense. Cynthia lives in the deep South, loves horror movies and has an addiction to chocolate. More information about Cynthia may be found at www.cynthiaeden.com.

Books by Cynthia Eden

Harlequin Intrigue

Killer Instinct
Abduction

The Battling McGuire Boys
Confessions
Secrets
Suspicions
Reckonings
Deceptions
Allegiances

Shadow Agents: Guts and Glory
Undercover Captor
The Girl Next Door
Evidence of Passion
Way of the Shadows

MIRA Books

Killer Instinct
The Gathering Dusk (prequel to *Abduction*)

Visit the Author Profile page at Harlequin.com for more titles.

CAST OF CHARACTERS

Jillian "Jill" West—FBI special agent Jill West has reached her breaking point. Once an elite member of the FBI's CARD (Child Abduction Rapid Deployment) team, she's now retreating back to her home along the Florida coast because she's worked too many cases that ended in tragedy.

Hayden Black—Former SEAL Hayden Black was the town bad boy until one desperate act changed the course of his life...and Jill's. For years he's worked to prove that he can be a hero, and when Jill comes back to town, he swears that he won't let her slip from his life again.

Christy Anderson—Years ago, Christy Anderson was abducted and killed in Hope, Florida. Her disappearance shattered Jill. When Jill returns to Hope, she vows to solve this cold case. But Jill doesn't realize the man who took Christy is still hunting in the coastal town...

Kurt Anderson—Kurt doesn't want Jill digging into the past. His sister is dead and gone, and he doesn't believe that anyone should disturb the dead. He'll do anything necessary to make sure his family is left to their grief.

Theodore Anderson—Theodore blames Jill for his daughter's disappearance. He has no intention of cooperating with her or the new sheriff in town. Theodore believes the past should stay dead. There is nothing but pain to be found by looking back.

Samantha Dark—When another young girl disappears in Hope, Florida, Jill calls in her friend Samantha for help. Samantha has profiled killers at the FBI, and she's determined to help find the perp—and rescue the missing girl.

Prologue

"Stay away from him, Jill." Jillian West's grandmother pointed toward the end of the long, wooden pier. A boy was there, gazing out at the distant waves, a boy who appeared to be just a little older than Jill. "He's trouble."

But he didn't look like trouble. The boy's blond hair blew in the wind and his faded T-shirt fluttered in the breeze.

"I'll only be inside a minute," her grandmother promised as she patted Jill's shoulder. "Stay here."

And then her grandmother was gone. She'd drifted into the little souvenir shop that waited near the pier, her voice drifting back to Jill as her grandmother called out a greeting to her friend inside the store.

Her grandmother had a lot of friends in Hope, Florida. It seemed that everyplace they went she met someone she knew. Jillian's flip-flops slid over the wooden pier as she stared up at the boy with the blond hair. She'd moved in with her grandmother just a few weeks before, but she still hadn't gotten a chance to talk with any kids in the town.

Her grandmother knew plenty of people, just no one who was close to Jillian's age. No other kids around thirteen for her to chat with as she adjusted to her sudden, jarring new life.

Just then, the boy glanced back at her. She stiffened, but then Jill found herself lifting her hand in an awkward wave. She even took a few quick steps toward him. His head cocked as he stared at her.

Her hand fell back to her side.

He's trouble. Her grandmother's warning whispered through her mind once more.

But he was coming closer to her. His sneakers didn't even seem to make a sound as he eliminated the distance between them, and then he was there, peering down at her. He was taller than she was, his shoulders already becoming broad, and he used one careless hand to shove back his overly long hair.

"I don't know you," he said. His voice was deeper than she'd expected. He appeared to be around fifteen, maybe sixteen, but that voice was so grown-up.

"No, ah, I'm new." She tucked her hands behind her back. "I'm Jillian, but my friends call me Jill."

His gaze swept over her—dark brown eyes. Deep eyes. When she looked hard enough—and Jill was looking so hard that she felt herself blush—she saw a circle of gold in those brown eyes.

"You think we're friends, Jill?" He emphasized her name, just a bit.

She shrugged. "We could be." She bit her lip and offered her hand to him. "It's nice to meet you."

He frowned at her hand, staring at it a little too long and hard, and then his gaze slowly rose to her face. "You have no clue who I am, do you?"

He's trouble. Jillian shook her head. She felt so silly standing there, with her hand offered to him. Maybe she should drop her hand.

"I'm not very good friend material." His lips twisted. "Ask anyone."

She dropped her hand. She felt her cheeks burn with embarrassment. *He doesn't want to be my friend.*

"I saw you with your grandmother."

Wait, when had he seen her? She'd thought that he'd been staring at the water the whole time she'd been chatting with her grandmother.

His head cocked. "I'm surprised she didn't tell you to stay away from me."

"She did," Jill blurted.

Surprise flashed on his face. "So you're not good at doing what you're told, huh?" He made a tut-tut sound. "What would your parents say?"

Her skin iced. The pain was so raw and fresh—it gutted her. Jill sucked in a sharp breath and took a quick step back. "They can't say anything. They're dead." And she shouldn't be talking to him. She shouldn't be so desperate for a friend, for *any* friend, that she'd disobey her grandmother. Her grandmother was all she had left. If her grandmother got mad at her…what if her grandmother decided she didn't want to be saddled with a kid? What if she dumped Jill someplace else? What if—

Jill spun on her heel. "I have to go." She ran away from him, nearly losing a flip-flop in her hurry. She'd go back to the car. Wait there. And she would not talk to *anyone* until her grandmother finished her chat. Her eyes stung with tears as she fled and Jill heard the boy call out her name.

But she didn't stop.

What would your parents say?

She wished they could still say something to her. Say *anything* to her.

The pier ended. Her flip-flops sank into the beautiful white sand of the beach, sand so white it was like sugar. The first time she'd seen that sand, she'd grabbed it, laughing at how light it felt as it ran through her fingers. She wasn't laughing now.

She swiped at the tears on her cheeks. The first kid she'd met, and she'd started crying in front of him. What a way to get a good reputation in the town. *Jillian's a crybaby. Jillian's a baby.*

Her grandmother's dependable four-door sedan waited a few feet away. There were only a few other cars in the parking lot. It was late, nearing sunset, and not many folks were still out.

"Are you okay, little girl?"

I'm not little. Those were the words that rose to her lips. But she didn't snap them at the man who approached her. He was frowning, looking concerned.

Probably because I'm crying.

"Are you all alone?" He seemed horrified by the very idea.

"M-my grandmother is in the souvenir shop." She pointed behind her. The man stepped closer to her. "She'll be out soon."

The man nodded as if that were a good thing, then his hand clamped over her shoulder. Hard. Hard enough to hurt and he leaned in toward Jill and whispered, "Not soon enough, Jill."

How does he know my name?

She opened her mouth, but Jill didn't get to

scream. He slapped his other hand over her mouth and yanked her against him. She kicked out, struggling, but he was big and strong. So much bigger than she was. And he was running with her, heading toward a van a few feet away.

No, no, this can't happen!

"Don't make me kill you now," he growled.

Jill froze.

He opened the side door of the van. He threw her inside, but Jill lunged forward, ready to jump back out again.

He hit her. A hard punch right to her face. It was the first time in Jill's life that she'd ever been hit. For a moment, she was dazed. Her gaze slid away from the man before her—a monster—and...

She saw him...the boy from the pier. The boy with the too long blond hair. He was running toward her.

"Jill!" the boy yelled.

But the man who'd grabbed her...he jabbed something into her neck. Something sharp. *A needle?*

She fell back into the van, her head hitting the side panel, and darkness flooded Jill's vision.

"Jill? Jill!"

Her eyes flew open and Jill sucked in a quick breath so that she could scream.

"No, don't." A sweaty hand flew over her mouth. "If you scream, he'll hear you and he'll find us."

Us?

Jill blinked as she became aware of her surroundings. She was in a room with no furniture, just wooden walls. Her hands—her hands were tied together and so were her feet. She was on a dirty, dusty floor. Light burned from overhead, too bright, too stark.

"We can't let him find us, Jill," the boy said.

Boy. It was the boy from the pier. He had scratches on his face and his eyes were wide and intense as he stared down at her.

"I'll untie you, and then we're going to run. We're going to run as fast as we can, got it?"

She nodded, tears stinging her eyes.

His hand slipped away from her mouth and he began to work on the ropes that held her. The ropes at her feet gave way quickly, but the ones that bound her wrists—they were knotted, stuck.

"Forget it," he said and yanked her up to her feet. "We'll get them later, *after* we're out of here."

She didn't even know where *here* was, but she wanted to leave. She wanted to leave right then.

He pushed her toward the window. It was open and the scent of the salty ocean blew in toward her. "I'll give you a boost. You get out, and you

go, got it? You *move*. You don't look back at me.
Trust me, I'll be coming. I'll be right behind you.
You just go."

Jill nodded. She'd go.

He pushed her through the window and she
fell out on the other side, hitting her shoulder
with a jarring impact, but Jill pounced back to
her feet and she started running. Only...there
didn't seem to be anywhere to run to. It was dark
and there were trees shooting up all around her, a
marshy-like area and she looked back, scared—

He was there. The boy with the too long hair.
He grabbed her bound wrists. "Come *on*, Jill."

She didn't see the man who'd taken her. She
was afraid he was out there, watching them. That
he was going to attack them. Going to hurt them
both.

Kill them.

They ran into muddy water, and it was cold,
chilling her. Her teeth started to chatter, not
from the cold, but from the terror clawing at
her. "H-he...hurt me." Her jaw still ached. "He...
took me..." Kidnapped her from right out in the
open. A parking lot.

"I saw him." His fingers fumbled with the
ropes that bound her wrists. The knots came free
and he rubbed at her skin, being so careful with
her. "I wasn't going to let you vanish."

Vanish.

That's what would have happened to her, Jill knew it. She just would have vanished without a trace. "I want to go home," she whispered.

Home...

The house she'd shared with her parents in Georgia. Her haven. Her safe place. She wanted her mom. She wanted her dad. She wanted this to be a terrible nightmare.

But the boy wrapped his arms around her and he held her tight. "It's okay. We're going to be okay."

She believed him. He'd found her, someway. Gotten her out of...there. He saved her. "I don't... I don't even know your name."

He pulled back and stared at her. "I'm Hayden. Hayden Black."

Hayden. Such a good name for a best friend.

They ran until they reached the road. They ran and ran, but each time a car came by, Hayden made her hide.

He was afraid the kidnapper was coming for them.

Hours ticked by and then they finally made it to the small sheriff's station. Lights blazed from inside the square building and patrol cars filled the parking lot. Hayden's fingers were laced with hers as they walked up the wooden steps that led to the station. He opened the door, and they slipped inside.

There was instant silence. Every eye turned toward them.

Jill looked down at herself. Her clothes were torn and muddy. She'd lost her flip-flops. Her feet were raw and blistered.

And she was sure her jaw was bruised. It still hurt so much.

"Jillian!" Her grandmother ran to her and yanked Jill close in a crushing hug. "My little Jilly!"

Jilly. Her mother used to call her that, too. *Jilly went up the hilly...* Her own version of the rhyme.

The tears were falling again. Jill couldn't stop them. Her grandmother wasn't mad. She wasn't going to send her away. Her grandmother smelled like sweet vanilla. Like apricots.

Like home.

"What in the hell did you do, boy?" It was a man's voice, rough and demanding. And that voice...the man...he was nearby. A big, bear-like man wearing a sheriff's uniform and sporting a gleaming badge. "You took that poor girl? You hurt her?"

No, no, of course Hayden hadn't hurt her. Jillian struggled out of her grandmother's desperate embrace. That big man had grabbed Hayden. His face was angry as the sheriff snarled, "You're just like your father."

All of the color bled from Hayden's face.

"You pulled the wrong stunt today," the man snapped. "You—"

Jill pushed her way between the sheriff and Hayden. Her whole body was shaking. "Hayden is my friend."

Pity flashed on the sheriff's face as his gaze peered down at her, lingering on her jaw. "Sweetheart, why don't you just relax with your grandmother? You don't have to be afraid. You don't—"

"Hayden saved me." Her dirty hand reached back and grabbed Hayden's. She held him tight. "A man...took me...from the pier parking lot." Her words were whispered and terror clawed at her as she remembered those desperate moments. "H-he hurt me. Tied me up. But Hayden got me out... Hayden helped me." *Hayden saved me.*

The only sound she could hear was the ticking of the big clock on the wall. Jill's desperate gaze flew around the room.

Her grandmother was crying.

The sheriff who'd been yelling at Hayden was staring at her in shock. And...

"I can take you back to him," Hayden said, his voice oddly calm and still sounding so deep and...strong. "When he took Jill from the pier, I followed him on a bike. I wrecked it near the cabin, smashed it good. So we had to run on foot to get back, but I remember everything about the place. I can take you there."

AND HE DID.

Hayden led the cops back to that little cabin that was nestled near the marsh. The authorities went in with sirens screaming and guns blazing. Jill sat huddled in the back of a patrol car, her grandmother's arms constricted around her. Hayden was beside them looking watchful, intense.

The sheriff and his deputies searched the cabin. They brought in dogs to track the man who'd been there, but he was long gone...

"It's okay, Jill," Hayden whispered.

Her head turned toward him.

"I'll make sure you stay safe."

Such a big promise but...

She believed him.

Hayden Black wasn't trouble. Her grandmother had been wrong about him.

He was a hero.

And he was her friend. Her very best friend in the whole entire world.

Chapter One

The world was dark and twisted. It was filled with monsters and evil.

FBI special agent Jill West kept a strong grip on her service weapon as she rushed into the little house at the end of Clover Lane. Her teammates were with her, moving quickly, efficiently. They were the agents on the Southeastern Division of CARD, the Child Abduction Rapid Deployment team, and their job was to find missing children.

Or in this specific case…one missing child. A sixteen-year-old girl named Jessica Thomas. Jessica had been gone for three days, but they'd tracked her abductor to this location, they'd followed their leads, they'd raced against time and now…

Be alive. Please, please, be alive.

There were too many cases that ended in tragedy, in funerals with grief-stricken families. Funerals with mothers and fathers who were too devastated to even speak. Her team needed a win...because those tragedies were pushing them all too close to the breaking point.

"Stay the hell back!" A man ran from the back room of that little house, a bloody knife gripped in his hand. "You ain't taking her from me! No one's taking her from me!"

In that instant, Jill realized three very important things.

One...the knife had recently been used on someone. The screaming man before her showed no injuries, so odds were high that the perp had attacked Jessica.

Two...the jerk was definitely on something. His speech was slurred, and he was weaving as he staggered toward her and the other agents in their bulletproof vests.

And three...this man wasn't going down easy. He was lunging forward to attack her—

"Stand down!" Jill yelled. "Drop the weapon, *now!*"

He didn't. He just screamed louder and lurched toward her.

Jill fired. Not a kill shot, she'd never taken that shot yet, but a shot that blasted into the man's right shoulder. The knife fell to the floor with a clatter as he screamed and his blood soaked his shirt. "Perp down," Jill snapped. She was wired—all of the agents were—and her ear-piece had a microphone that would pick up her words so she knew the agent monitoring the team would immediately dispatch medical personnel. Then she hurried forward, kicking the knife even farther out of his way.

Agent Henry Shaw was at her side. He kept his gun leveled at the man howling on the floor. Henry, a tall, distinguished African-American agent, was the leader of their team. A damn good leader. "I got this guy, Jill," Henry told her, his eyes never leaving the perp. "Find the girl."

Jill gave an abrupt nod and hurried to the back room. She kept her gun at the ready. All of their intel had indicated that they were only looking for one assailant, that Neal Matthew Patrick had become obsessed with the sixteen-year-old victim after first meeting her in an online chat room. He'd abducted her, determined to live out that obsession.

But just in case the guy did have a partner, in case someone else was waiting to attack in that back room, Jill didn't lower her guard.

The door was partially open. She used her foot to swing it all the way inward and then—

"Help...me..." Such a weak whisper, completely at odds with the desperate howling coming from Neal.

Jessica was on the floor, her hands pressing

to her stomach—trying to stem the heavy flow of blood that had already soaked her shirt. Her face was stark white, her eyes so big and scared in her young face.

"Victim needs assistance!" Jill called out, knowing the monitoring agent would act immediately. "Get help in here, now!" And Jill ran to the girl's side. She needed to see just how bad the damage was but the fear in her heart already told her…

Bad…it's too bad.

"I—I want…m-my mom…" Jessica whispered.

Jill looked at the wounds—multiple stab wounds. So deep. A pool of blood was under Jessica's body. "We'll take you to your mom, don't you worry, okay?" She applied pressure, fear nearly choking her.

"I'm sorry…" Jessica's voice was even softer now. She was starting to shake. "T-tell her… s-sorry…n-never…should have…g-gone…"

Because Jessica had made a date with Neal. She'd snuck out of her house to meet him at her high school football field. She hadn't realized she was going to meet a man who'd long gone over the edge. She couldn't have known how dangerous that meeting would be for her. *Just a date. A sixteen-year-old going on a date.* That was all it had been, to Jessica.

"It's all right," Jill told her. "You'll be with your mom soon and you can—"

Footsteps rushed behind her. Help, finally coming. The EMTs ran into the room and pushed Jill back. She watched them, hoping, praying, so very desperate.

Jessica was shaking even harder now.

Jill looked down at her hands. The girl's blood covered her fingers. Her hands fisted. Her breath heaved in and out. Every heartbeat that passed seemed to echo in her ears.

Jill was still standing there, still watching them, when Jessica's eyes closed, when the girl took her last breath. The EMTs didn't give up, they kept trying to work, kept trying to bring her back but...

Jessica's body had gone still.

She had just...

Another victim. Another child taken.

Jill stumbled outside, her stomach in knots. The night air hit her face, slightly chilled, making goose bumps rise on her arms. The cases weren't supposed to be like this. She was supposed to help, not arrive in time to see a young girl die.

Tears pricked her eyes. The perp—that jerk Neal—was in the back of a nearby ambulance. He was alive. He was yelling at the agents with him.

Jessica was gone. Life was so unfair. So cold

and dark and violent. She looked at the scene around her, the chaos, the pain, and then Jill glanced down at the blood that covered her hands.

I have to get away. I can't do this. Not anymore.

"Jill?"

She put her hands behind her back and glanced over to see Henry frowning at her. Henry had been her mentor from the moment she signed on to the team. He'd trained her from day one when she joined CARD. As he stared at her, she saw the pity in his dark eyes.

He knows I'm close to breaking.

"We'll need to tell the parents," Jill said, trying to make her voice sound strong. The mother. They'd have to tell the mother. Jill swallowed.

"I can do it," Henry offered. He always handled the families so well. He seemed to know exactly what to say to them. How to give them sympathy. How to let them grieve. "You did good work on this case," he told her, his voice soft. "You were the one to find the house, to trace Neal here, you were—"

"I was too late." That was the stark truth.

"*This* time," Henry said, his jaw tightening. "But there will be other cases, other children. You of all people know how important our job is."

Because of her past, yes, she knew. She also

knew… "I have to talk to Jessica's mother." She needed to look the woman in the eyes and tell her that at the end, Jessica had been thinking of her. That her daughter had loved *her*. When she took a case, Jill saw it through to the end. But after she met with the Thomas family… Jill's breath shuddered out. "Then I think I'll take some of that vacation time I've been saving." Hoarding, more like. Work had become her life in the last few years. Only now, that life seemed to be tearing her apart.

"Good idea," Henry murmured. "Maybe you can go someplace warm. Someplace where you can forget about this coldness for a time."

She thought of Jessica's last words. "I think I'm going home," Jill said. Home. The spot of her greatest happiness…

And her most desperate moments.

HE SAW HER the instant she came into town. It wasn't as if it were easy to miss a woman like her. Jill West had always been able to stand out in a crowd. The sunlight hit her dark red head, making it gleam. She wore a pair of jeans that hugged her long legs, and she walked with an easy grace as she headed toward the pier.

Hayden Black stood inside of the bait shop, watching her as she moved with such purpose.

It had been far too long since he'd seen Jill...
Too damn long.

What were the odds that when she came back
to Hope, he spotted her on that same damn pier?
He hadn't thought that she *would* come back.
Hell, he'd been planning a trip to see her in
Georgia, but for her to show up now...in that
spot...

He'd never been a particularly lucky guy. The
luckiest day of his life had been when he'd met
a cute redheaded girl on that same pier.

A girl with the greenest eyes he'd ever seen.
A girl who'd turned one of the most hated punks
in that town into a hero.

"You gonna watch her all day?" Jeff Mazo,
the owner of the bait shop asked. "Or are you
actually gonna go over there and tell that woman
hello?"

Jeff didn't get it. The woman in question
might not exactly be thrilled to see him. He and
Jill hadn't ended things on the best of terms.

*I lusted for her during my teens. When I
became a man, she was all that I could think
about...*

Then she'd joined the FBI and he'd become a
SEAL. Two different paths. Two different lives.

Now they were back. Both back in Hope.

Maybe it's not luck. Maybe it was more than
that. Maybe.

"Never realized you were the nervous sort," Jeff snorted, as if he'd just found this discovery incredibly amusing. "Bet that made for some real interesting missions, huh?"

Hayden just shook his head, refusing to let the guy needle him. "Don't worry, Jeff, I'm just planning my move." More like hoping that Jill didn't tell him to get the hell away from her. He gave a little wave. "See you later, buddy."

He headed out on the pier, and the old wood was sturdy beneath his feet. The scent of salt water tickled his nose. *Hope.* The town was gorgeous, a sweet little hideaway on the Florida Gulf Coast. It was early spring, so the place hadn't gotten overwhelmed with tourists, not yet. Sure, a few hours away, the college kids were running amok at some of the bigger beachside cities, but Hope was quieter.

Softer.

Nothing ever happened in Hope.

Except for the abduction of a sweet redheaded girl...

The man who'd taken Jill had never been caught. And Hayden... For years, he'd woken up from nightmares in a cold sweat because of that fact. He'd been so worried that someone would take Jill from him.

And in the end, I'm the one who lost her. I did that all on my own.

He marched toward her. The wind ruffled her T-shirt and her hair, but she didn't seem to care. She kept staring out at the waves, turbulent swells because a storm was coming.

When he was just a few feet away from her, Hayden stopped. "Hello, Jill."

She didn't whirl toward him in surprise. Didn't give any shocked explanation. That wasn't Jill's style. Instead, she slowly turned to him with a look in her guarded green gaze that said she'd known all along that she was being watched.

But her green eyes widened just the faintest bit, a small show of surprise that told him... Jill *had* expected someone else to be on that pier. She just hadn't expected that someone to be him.

"Hayden?" Her delicate brows arched as her gaze swept over him. "What are you doing here?"

He gave her a small smile even as he stalked a bit closer to her. That was the thing about Jill, she always made him want to get closer. Always pulled him in, even when he knew he should be staying away from her. Mingled with the scent of the ocean, he caught her fragrance. Sweet vanilla.

"I could ask you the same question," he murmured. Damn but she looked good. Better than good. Heart-shaped face, wide eyes, full lips. She had just the faintest hint of freckles across the top of her nose, a little bit of the girl she'd been still hanging on to the woman she'd become.

She took a step toward him and her hands lifted, as if she'd reach out and hug him. Once, she would have done that. Once, she would have run right into his arms and held him tight.

And she would have fit perfectly against him. The way she always had.

But she faltered. Her hands fell. Uncertainty flashed on her face. "I'm here for a vacation. Isn't that why most folks come to Hope?"

It wasn't why he was back in Hope, and he didn't believe for an instant that it was why she was back there, either.

His gaze swept over her. Jill was definitely grown-up now. She stood close to five foot six, and that meant his six-foot-three frame towered over her. When they'd been kids, she'd joked and asked him when he'd ever stop growing.

Every good memory I have is tied up in Jill West. So he didn't stop, he didn't falter. He closed the last bit of distance between them and wrapped her in a hug. Probably too tight, but he couldn't really help himself. It had been far too long since he'd seen Jill. Even longer since he'd held her.

She still fit him. Far too perfectly. His arms slid around her back and he pulled her close. Her scent wrapped around him and reminded him of all that he'd missed. Too many years away from Jill.

Too many mistakes. And—

She was hugging him back. A quick tightening of her arms around him as if she were just as glad to see him. His heart thudded in his chest. Maybe it wasn't too late. Maybe he hadn't screwed things to hell and back between them. Maybe—

She stopped hugging him. "Let me go," Jill said, her voice soft.

He did. The same way he'd let her go before, ten years ago. She'd been nineteen. He'd been twenty-one.

His hands slid away from her. "Still as beautiful as ever."

She frowned. Right, Jill never liked to be told she was beautiful. It made her uncomfortable.

"Am I supposed to say that you're still as handsome as ever?" Her head cocked and her gaze swept over him. "You are. But I'm sure plenty of women tell you that."

No other woman was Jill. *His* Jill.

"Mr. Navy SEAL." She smiled, but the smile was just a twist of her lips. No gleam appeared in her eyes and her expression didn't lighten. He'd always worked so hard to make her give him a grin—worked even harder to hear her laugh.

"Shouldn't you be out defending the world? Working those secret missions?"

Actually… "I'm not active duty any longer." He'd given ten years of his life to service. Now… now he knew exactly what he wanted to do with the years he had left. "I just bought a house here in Hope."

He heard her quick exhale. Ah, so he *had* surprised her.

"And here I thought you liked traveling the world. You wanted to see everything, remember?" She turned away. "But now you're back here."

He reached for her hand. "And I thought you wanted to save the world." No, he knew she'd wanted to save children, kids who'd been just like her.

Taken.

Stolen.

"So what's a hotshot FBI agent like you doing in a small town like this?" His index finger slid along her inner wrist, a careless caress.

Or maybe a very careful one. Even he wasn't sure about that.

"Hiding." And this time, her smile broke what was left of his heart. "Because I'm really not so much of a hotshot." She looked down at their hands. "I've got too much blood on me."

Alarm pulsed through him. "Jill?"

"Let me go," she said once more.

Another caress, a gentle touch right over her rapid pulse point, and his hand slid away from her.

"I need to head home," she said, then seemed to catch herself. "Head to the cabin. I rented a place on the beach. The beach is supposed to be good for the soul, right?"

He wouldn't know. The only thing that had ever been good for his soul...well, that was Jill. She'd changed him, though he didn't think she realized just how much. He didn't think Jill even realized how influential she'd been in his life.

She'd always thought that he'd saved her.

Oh, baby, that could not be further from the truth.

She slipped by him and started walking toward the parking lot.

"Jillian West." Her name pulled from him.

She hesitated.

"We're not kids any longer."

Jill glanced over her shoulder. "I haven't been a child since I was thirteen years old."

No, she hadn't been. He knew that. One terrible act had changed her world.

"I came back to Hope for many reasons," Hayden said. Maybe she deserved that warning. "I didn't expect to see you so soon."

"So soon? Why expect to see me at all?"

Ah, now that was just cold. "Do you ever think about us?"

She faced the front again. "I try not to."

He took that hit straight on his heart. "Really? Because I pretty much think about you every single day." Though the nights were the worst. When he'd been fighting, when he'd been in one hell after another, memories of Jill had always come to him at night.

But a memory wasn't walking away from him right then. No memory, no ghost.

He'd watched her walk away before, but this time, things were going to be different. This time, he was fighting for Jill.

She just didn't realize it yet.

He wasn't the town troublemaker any longer. Wasn't the boy who'd never been good enough for Jillian West. Now he was back in Hope to prove himself to the person who mattered the most.

To you, Jill. For you. I'm back for you.

HE'D NEVER BELIEVED in coincidences. His life didn't work that way. Everything that happened was part of fate.

So when he saw the redheaded woman walking off the pier, the light glinting in her hair, the sunset hitting her just right…

He remembered another time.

A girl, not a woman. A girl who'd been walking alone. Who'd been coming right to him.

He'd had such plans for that girl. So many grand, wonderful plans.

But she'd left him. Ran away. Escaped before he could enjoy himself. Such a shame. In all of his years of hunting, she'd been the only one to escape.

His one failure. The failure that had changed everything for him.

THE REDHEADED WOMAN was coming closer to him, nearing the parking lot, so he cranked up his Jeep and drove away. As he left, he saw two young girls riding their bikes. So many kids enjoyed riding their bike in that area. There were many trails. Tons of paths.

So many places to vanish.

One of the girls had blond hair. The other had dark brown locks.

Pity one of them doesn't have red hair. Because, quite suddenly, he was seeing red in his mind. The red hair of a victim.

The red of blood.

He hadn't planned to ever hunt again in Hope. But…seeing that redheaded woman…

There are no coincidences. Maybe she was there, at that time, for a reason.

Maybe…

Chapter Two

She had a serious problem on her hands, Jill knew it. She was on Day Two of her vacation—*Day Two*—and she was heading toward the local sheriff's office. She should have been walking on a beach, riding a bike, reading a book, something…anything but…

Anything but looking for a case. She had so many issues. The plan had been to head home to Hope in order to relax, to get her mind off death.

Instead, she couldn't stop thinking about the missing.

She pushed open the door to the sheriff's office. A bell jingled over her head. It was quiet inside, she heard the hum of an air conditioner, the ticking of a clock and—

"Hello, there, Jill. Didn't expect to see you again so soon."

His voice. Dark and deep and rumbly. Jill had

often thought that Hayden Black had a voice like whiskey—it just got better with age.

Sexier.

Her gaze slid to the right and she saw him. Hayden was smiling at her, that teasing half smile that too many women had admired. His dark eyes glinted at her as he stood in the doorway—the doorway that led directly into Sheriff Ronald Peek's inner sanctum. Only...

She didn't see Sheriff Peek. The big, rather bearlike older man was nowhere to be seen.

She *did* see Hayden...and his brown sheriff's uniform. The guy even had a gleaming, gold star pinned to his chest. *No way.* "You have got to be kidding me." Jill glanced around the little station again. No one else was there. Seriously?

"Kidding?" Hayden straightened. "Why? Don't you think I look good in this uniform?"

Her lips thinned. *Good* didn't even come close to describing the man and he knew it. Hayden's shoulders stretched far and wide, making the uniform shirt strain at the seams. He was tall and powerful, and he should *not* have been standing there.

Mostly because she wasn't quite up to handling Hayden. He'd always been able to see right through the mask that she tried to wear in order to hide her emotions. Considering how hollowed out she felt on the inside, the last thing

Jill wanted was for Hayden to glimpse her weakness. She cleared her throat. "I'm here to see Sheriff Peek."

He winced and straightened away from the doorway. "Good luck with that, sweetheart—er, I mean, Jill."

She glowered at him.

"Peek retired about a month ago. Took off for Alaska. Apparently, facing the last great American frontier has always been a dream for him." Hayden's lips twitched. "And, it, uh, seems he'd been watching a lot of TV about building a cabin in the Alaskan wilderness. The call of the wild definitely got to old Ron." Hayden rolled back his shoulders. "You're looking at the new sheriff."

She shook her head.

He nodded. "Sheriff Hayden Black, at your service."

"You...you can't be sheriff. Was there a vote or—"

"Special appointment," he murmured. "Ron gave me his highest recommendation, and, believe it or not, the folks in this town seemed happy to have me take the job."

Jill's breath heaved out. "Of course, they're happy to have you. I have no doubt that you'll be an asset here."

Surprise flashed on his face.

"What?" Now her lips pulled down. "You think because of our, uh, past, that I wouldn't support you? You're a good man, Hayden." And maybe she'd gotten a few glimpses of his case files from his overseas work. Some days, she'd wondered about him. She'd worried. When she'd first read his mission files and seen just how dangerous his SEAL work was, Jill had been terrified.

Knowing that he wasn't hers any longer... she'd tried to keep her emotional distance. That had been impossible.

He took a step toward her. "You know folks in this town didn't always think that way. I had to prove—"

She held up her hand. "Stop it, Hayden. You never had to prove anything to me. I hope you know that."

His mouth tightened.

The bell jingled behind her. Jill looked back and saw a young deputy saunter inside the station. He had black hair and blue eyes and when he saw her, he came to a quick stop— and he tightened his grip on the doughnut bag in his hand. "Uh, a visitor? A case?" His eyes seemed to light up. "Ma'am, do you need assistance?" He hurried toward the check-in desk and plunked down his bag. "I'm Deputy Finn Patrick, and I can—"

"She's not here for business, Finn," Hayden muttered. "It's personal."

A tingle snaked up Jill's spine. *Personal.* Once upon a time, things had been very, very personal between them. When she looked at Hayden, the memories slid through her mind. She figured all of the stories she'd heard over the years were true—a woman never forgot her first love.

Especially when that love happened to be a guy like Hayden Black.

But now Finn was looking at her with speculation in his eyes. Hope was a small town—very, very small. And the last thing she wanted was for gossip to start spreading about her hooking up with the new sheriff. Jill reached into her bag and pulled out her ID. "Actually, I'm here to talk about an old case."

Finn's eyes doubled in size. "You're FBI!"

"Yes."

Finn appeared absolutely thrilled.

"What case?" Hayden asked, his voice a low growl. "When I saw you yesterday, you didn't mention a case."

"And you didn't mention that you were the sheriff, either."

Hayden sauntered closer. He leaned in and said, voice soft, "That's because you ran before I had the chance to tell you."

She wanted to tell him that she didn't run—

not from anything or anyone, but those words would have been a lie. After all, wasn't she in Hope because she was running? From all the death that seemed to stalk her? She stared into his eyes and said the name that she knew haunted them both, "Christy Anderson."

His jaw tightened.

"Christy who?" Finn asked.

Hayden curled his fingers around her arm. "FBI special agent Jillian West and I will be talking in my office, Finn." His voice had gone flat and cold as he steered her toward the open doorway.

"It was nice to meet you, Agent West!" Finn called out.

She glanced back and saw that he'd opened his bag of doughnuts. The scent of glaze drifted to her, but then she was inside of Hayden's office, and he shut the door with a very distinct click.

"What in the hell are you planning?" Hayden asked her.

She pulled her arm from his grip. "I'm planning on solving a cold case." Because maybe that case was one of the many demons that plagued her. Maybe if she could solve that case…maybe if she could give the family some closure…then every time she lost a victim with the FBI, she wouldn't feel so lost inside.

Maybe.

Maybe not.

"Did the FBI send you down here to research Christy Anderson's case?"

"No, I came down here because I knew it was time to face my own past. You can only hide from the truth for so long." Her smile felt bittersweet. "After all, you and I both know…we traded my life for Christy's."

He swore and advanced toward her.

Jill threw up her hands. "Don't! I don't want you touching me, okay, Hayden?"

He flinched, as if she'd hurt him, and Jill realized that she had. *Right. Like he never hurt me.* One night…ten years ago…he'd ripped her heart right out of her chest.

A woman could do a whole lot in this world without a heart.

"You used to like it when I touched you," Hayden said.

Oh, no, he had *not* just gone there. Jill's hands went to her hips. "And you used to not be a jerk who turned his back on the *one* person he swore mattered the most to him—"

Pain flashed on his face. "Jill—"

"No!" She squeezed her eyes shut. "This isn't what I want." It wasn't. And she wasn't just hurting Hayden. She was hurting herself. Jill forced her eyes to open. "I'm sorry." Time to be incredibly honest. "I didn't count on seeing you again."

Actually, she'd been sure he was an ocean away. So much for her contact at the CIA. Mr. Oh, Yes, I Know Where His SEAL Team Is. "I wasn't prepared for you, and I'm..." Her laughter held a rough edge. "I was already raw enough before I came to Hope."

"Believe me, Jill. The last thing I ever want is to hurt you."

He seemed so sincere. She wanted to believe him. "Maybe we can call a truce?"

His gaze drifted over her and turned wistful. "I didn't realize we were at war."

No? "I could use a friend right now." A stark admission. "I've... I've always thought you were my *best* friend." And that was why it had hurt her so much when he'd walked away. She hadn't just lost her lover. She'd lost her friend.

Did he have any clue...she'd used to imagine their wedding? She'd thought they would grow old together. That they would always be an un-stoppable team. Because that was how she'd felt when they were together. Unstoppable.

Safe.

She'd always been safe with Hayden. Then he'd ripped away her safety net.

"I will be anything you want me to be," Hayden promised, his voice a rumble.

Her stare lifted, held his. Did he know why she'd asked him not to touch her? Did he realize just what his touch did to her? Even the careless brush of his fingers over her arm had her tensing. His touch stirred her memories, stirred *her*. Her heartbeat raced, her breath hitched, and she ached…

For things that she couldn't have.

"Right now, I need you to be the sheriff who is cooperating with an FBI agent." Though she had zero jurisdiction. She wasn't going to point out that fact, though. "I'm in town, you have a cold case, and I want to see if there's anything I can do to help solve it."

The faint lines on either side of his mouth deepened. Time had been kind to Hayden. Gone were the boyish looks he'd had years ago. Now, his face was ruggedly handsome, carved and hard.

Sexy.

Especially when he smiled. Hayden didn't have dimples, definitely not. But he did have hard slashes that appeared in his cheeks when he let himself really smile. Once upon a time, his real smiles had been reserved for her.

A lifetime ago.

"Christy Anderson has been dead a long time, Jill," he spoke carefully.

"I know exactly how long Christy's been dead." She paced toward the window and looked out. She figured this had to be the only sheriff's office in the country with a view of the ocean. Talk about a prime spot. And, most days, it was a plum job, too. There wasn't a whole lot of crime in Hope. The occasional bar fight, some drunk and disorderly conduct…nothing too bad.

The last *bad* thing…well, that had happened to Jill. And to Christy. Because one day—*one day*—after Hayden and Jill escaped from that little cabin on the edge of the marsh, Christy Anderson had gone missing. Only no one had been there to follow the girl when she was abducted. No one had been there to get her out of that sick jerk's clutches.

And…less than twenty hours later, Christy's body had been found on the beach. She'd been found completely dry, covered with a blanket. She'd never touched the water.

Her neck had been broken. Left behind in the dark.

I lived, but she died. And that truth would never leave Jill alone.

"I want to find the man who killed her," Jill said, nodding her head as she stared out at the waves. Last night's storm lingered on the surf. "Because if I find him…"

"You'll find the man who took you."

Yes. And she'd stop always looking over her shoulder, always wondering… *Is he watching? Is he coming back?* An FBI agent was supposed to be confident, supposed to fear nothing and no one, but Jill feared far too much.

"You of all people know..." The floor creaked beneath his heavy footsteps. "The odds of finding him—after all this time—it's going to be nearly impossible."

She rolled her shoulders back in a shrug. "So maybe I'll dig into the files. Maybe I'll spend a few days of vacation searching for evidence that won't lead anywhere. It's my time to waste."

He was behind her. She could feel him. Jill made herself look back. "I need this, Hayden."

He nodded once, grimly. His hand lifted as if he'd touch her cheek, but then his fingers curled closed as he seemed to catch himself. His fisted hand fell back to his side. "Jill, when are you going to realize that I'd pretty much do anything for you?"

Shock radiated through her. He stalked toward the wide, cherrywood desk that sat in the middle of the office. He pushed the chair back and opened the top drawer. A moment later, he was lifting a yellowed file and offering it to her. "Not a lot is in here, I'm afraid."

She felt rooted to the spot. "You...you'd already pulled the file?" She knew there was an old records room in the back of the station. As a teen, she'd trailed after Sheriff Peek many times once she'd realized that she'd wanted to go into law enforcement. He'd said she was interning with him…and he'd strode around with his chest puffed out.

The first time she'd met Peek, he'd been tearing into Hayden. It was only later, much later, that she'd come to see the good heart hidden inside the hardened man. *And I came to learn just why he blamed Hayden that day.* Why so many in the town had.

"I pulled her file the day I took the job," Hayden answered.

Again, he'd surprised her. "Why?"

His lips twisted in his half smile, the smile that said he was holding back secrets. "Same reason you did. I want to catch the bastard."

Her heart thudded into her chest. Hayden wasn't the boy he'd been. Staring at him right then, she saw that his eyes had gone flat and cold, so hard and deadly with intent. This wasn't the boy she'd known or even the young man she'd loved.

This was the SEAL. Dangerous. Dark.

Almost…a stranger.

"He took you, Jill. *You.*" Hayden shook his head. "Do you think I have ever stopped wanting to catch him? I *won't* ever stop. I know he's still out there. He thinks he got away clean, but justice comes to everyone. Sooner or later."

She took the file from him. Her fingers brushed

his and a spark seemed to slip though her at that soft touch. She pulled back—too fast—and held the thin file carefully.

"You want to hunt him?" Hayden asked. "Fine, we'll hunt him. We'll do it together. This time, we aren't kids running in the dark."

No, they weren't.

"But be warned…there's not a lot of information in that file." His words were grim. "The guy didn't leave a whole lot of evidence behind. He knew what he was doing. He was smart."

The smart, organized killers were the most dangerous. "I've worked cold cases before," Jill told him. The CARD team members were focused exclusively on child abduction cases. When there was not an active case for them to investigate, then they often turned their attention to older crimes, hoping that they could find a piece of evidence that had been overlooked or that new technology would lead them in a new direction on a particular case. "I know that it's often like searching for a needle in a very giant haystack."

His dark gaze dropped to the thin folder. "That's a small haystack. Peek is a good man, but he was in way over his head with her case. See for yourself. There's an empty office down the hall you can use. Once you've read over the file, we can talk. Compare our thoughts."

She liked that he wasn't trying to influence her by saying what he might already suspect. She'd found that it was always better to go into an investigation without another agent's expectations or suspicions already in the open, those just tended to cloud the situation for her. She liked to see things with fresh eyes. "Thanks." She turned for the door.

Her hand was reaching for the doorknob when he said, "I missed you."

Her breath seemed to chill her lungs. "Did you?"

"Yes, I did." His voice was flat. Stark. Not hiding anything from her. "It's damn good to see you."

I missed you, too. She opened the door.

"I won't make the same mistake again."

Now she did glance back at him. On this, they needed to be very clear. She'd survived a broken heart once, courtesy of Hayden Black. "Neither will I." Then she left him.

It was better this way. Far, far better to just stick to the case.

HE KNEW THE REDHEAD. And he'd been right. Seeing her on the pier yesterday, in that exact same spot, at nearly the exact same time of evening… it hadn't been coincidence.

It had been fate.

Sixteen years ago, Jillian West had come to Hope, Florida. Quiet, withdrawn, her parents dead. She'd seemed to be his perfect prey. A gift delivered right to his doorstep.

He'd been following her for days before he approached her at the pier. He always liked to watch before he made his move. He had to be smart. So he'd watched and he'd acted at just the right moment.

Jillian had fought him, but he'd gotten her away. He'd had such plans for her, but when he went back to his cabin, she'd been gone.

Long gone. And his rage had nearly blinded him.

Jillian West.

The victim who'd gotten away. She'd stayed in town. Stayed until her grandmother died. Then the gossip he'd heard said that she'd joined the FBI. She'd wanted to help find missing children.

The folks in the little town had admired her.

He'd hated her.

Because of her, he'd lost *everything*. He'd had to be careful and to watch his steps. Had to hold back his impulses. Had to *lose* himself.

But then his life had changed yesterday, when he'd seen her.

Now he knew the real reason he'd stayed in Hope all these long years.

I knew—one day—we'd finish what we started.

It was time to act. Time to catch the only prey to ever get away from him. And then... only then...would his work truly be finished. He wasn't weak any longer. Finally, finally, he was strong. Better than ever.

The timing was perfect. For him.

He paused for just a moment outside of the sheriff's office. She was in there and he knew she wasn't alone. Hayden Black was close by, the way he always was when Jillian was near.

Tugging his baseball cap down, he turned away. As he headed toward the beach, he started to whistle. This was going to be different for him. Not as easy, more of a challenge. She was FBI. She'd had training.

But she wasn't better than him. Wasn't smarter. He'd been evading FBI agents for *years*. He had this down.

And Jillian...well, she was about to see what it was like to be prey again. *Only this time, you won't get away. I'll make sure there's no one there to save you, Jillian.*

He was getting his life back, and in order to do that, FBI agent Jillian West had to die.

Chapter Three

Hayden lifted his hand and rapped his knuckles against the door frame. At the sound, Jill's head whipped up and she blinked at him, a few dazed blinks, and he knew that she'd had herself fully immersed in the case file.

She'd made herself comfortable in the little office. She had a laptop open on the desk, positioned just to her right, and she'd started tacking some notes up on the bulletin board to her left. His eyebrows rose as he realized that she was certainly making the most of that slim file.

"Hayden?" She rose to her feet. "What's wrong?"

Not a damn thing. Finally, his world felt right. Because she was there. But he made a show of looking at his watch. "You've been in here for almost five hours. I thought you might want to take a lunch break with me."

"Five hours?" She seemed surprised and gave

a little laugh. "Sorry, I, um, tend to get a bit lost in my work."

He thought that might be an understatement.

She snapped her laptop shut. "But I would like some lunch…and a chance to pick your brain, now that I've had a chance to form my own impressions of the case." She grabbed her bag. "How about we just pick up some sandwiches and eat on the beach?"

They'd done that so many times as kids. Tossed a blanket on the sand. Stared at the waves, talked and dreamed. After Jill's abduction, her grandmother had gone through a phase where she was almost hypervigilant. She hadn't wanted to let Jill out of her sight. She hadn't let her granddaughter go anyplace but to school and right back home and…

Jill had turned reserved and quiet.

He'd gone to her grandmother and talked to her. He promised her that Jill would always be safe with him. And the lady…the lady had actually trusted *him*. She'd let Jill go on walks with him. Go to the beach with him.

Start to live again, with him.

They grabbed sandwiches from the deli next door, and then he snagged a blanket from the back of his SUV. Keeping a beach blanket handy was standard operating procedure for anyone who lived in Hope. The sunsets were not to be missed.

As they walked along the sand, Jill gave him a quick smile, a smile that actually reached her green eyes and made them gleam. "Just like old times, isn't it?"

Seagulls called overhead and the waves thundered as they hit the beach.

He stared at her a moment, and thought about the old times, the *best* times of his life. "Yes."

Her smile slipped. "Um, here, let me spread out the blanket." Jill eased it onto the sand, and then she sat down and he stared at her.

Jill was there, actually back with him. He was not going to mess this up. Hayden eased onto the blanket beside her and handed her one of the sandwiches. For a time, they ate in silence. He was far too conscious of her, beside him. The wind teased a lock of her hair and sent it dancing over her left cheek. He wanted to brush that hair back and tuck it behind her ear...but Jill had made it clear she didn't want him touching her.

Damn unfortunate, since touching her was the main thing he wanted.

"It doesn't make sense," Jill suddenly said. Her head turned and their eyes met. "Do you know how rare it is to have two girls taken within such a short period like that?"

Yeah, he did. He wasn't an expert on child

abduction like she was, but because of her, he'd definitely done his share of research.

"The fact that the guy stayed here and took Christy after I escaped…it suggests that he was acting out a compulsion. That he *had* to kidnap and—"

"Murder?" Hayden cut in.

She nodded. "Yes." Her gaze fell to the sand.

"There were never any other cases in Hope that fit his MO." That had been the very first thing Hayden checked once he came back to town. "No abductions at all. After that one weekend, Hope went back to its normal 3.5 drunk and disorderly arrests a year." He blew out a hard breath. "No more murders. No more missing children."

"Just one hellish weekend." She put her empty sandwich wrapper back in the bag and took a sip of bottled water. "It doesn't fit. In all the cases I've studied, a one-and-done situation like this… it's too rare. If the perp were following a compulsion, he would have needed to act again. Sure, there would be a cooling-off period but—"

"Whoa, whoa, hold on." He balled up his own wrapper and tossed it in the bag. "A 'cooling-off' period?" Hayden repeated. "That sounds like we're dealing with some kind of…of serial killer or something."

"There are serial abductors," Jill murmured.

"It's unfortunate, but it does occur. Most types of abductions are family abductions, but nonfamily abductions…well, there are different rules in place for those."

Rules? Okay, now this was just making him angrier.

"If this were a serial abductor we were looking at, there would have been more victims," Jill said. Her delicate jaw hardened. "The perp wouldn't have just vanished, just—just totally disappeared off the grid."

"Let's back up," Hayden directed. The waves rolled onto the shore. "Tell me what you believe happened to Christy, based on the report."

"That tiny five-page report? The one that contained zero DNA evidence or crime scene analysis?"

A definite edge had entered her voice. "Yeah, that one." He'd felt the same frustration that she was showing when he'd reviewed the material.

"I think the killer had done those same actions before. He knew how to clean up after himself. He knew how to make sure there wasn't so much as a sliver of evidence left behind. This definitely wasn't amateur hour."

"That's why you think we're looking at a serial."

"Her neck was broken. A personal, intimate death. That type of kill suggests that the perp wanted to have power over his victim. He liked the control." She nodded. "That's probably why he picked two young teen girls as his victims here in Hope—he thought we were weaker than he was, that he could control us both."

"You're profiling him."

She rolled back her shoulders and finally caught that lock of hair that had been teasing her cheek. "I've taken some profile classes at Quantico, yes, but that's not exactly my strong suit. You want someone who can get into a killer's head?" Her lips lifted once again in a faint smile. "That would be my friend Samantha. When it comes to killers, she's an absolute genius."

Hayden found himself leaning closer to Jill. "You're the one who saw him, face-to-face." He'd just seen the back of the jerk's head, his baseball cap, his dark shirt, his jeans as the guy ran toward the front of that old SUV. An SUV that had later been found, stripped down and abandoned, two towns over.

Her smile flickered. "I saw him, and I'm the one who should have been able to identify him. I know that."

"Jill, that's not what I—"

Sadness was heavy in her voice as she said, "I know Christy's parents blamed me."

His hand fisted on the sand.

"Did you know…they came to my grand-mother's house once?"

"What? You never said—"

"Her father had been drinking. Her mother was trying to keep him under control. He was yelling and saying that I could have stopped the killer. That I knew who he was. That it was my fault Christy was gone." Her lips turned down. "Kept saying I shouldn't be living when he was burying his daughter. That it wasn't right. That it was *my* fault."

"Why the hell didn't you tell me?" He jumped to his feet.

She tilted back her head and stared up at him. "Because I thought he was right. It was my fault. If I could have remembered more about the guy, if I could have described him better—"

"Jill," he cut in, growling her name, and then he reached for her—breaking that no-touching rule—and hauled her up beside him. "Nothing that happened was your fault. You were a victim. Just that. You didn't do anything wrong."

The wind blew against them.

"I remembered he was wearing big sunglasses, and a baseball hat. He had a square jaw, and I think I saw a little bit of blond hair on the side of his head, peeking from beneath the hat." He heard the faint click of her swallow. "He was tall, over six feet, I believe. And I remember thinking that he was far too strong."

Hayden hated that man. *Hated him.*

"Peek tried to get me to do a sketch," Jill said, "but that sketch could have been anyone. When the artist was done, I didn't even recognize the picture I was staring at." She gave a little laugh, one that sounded bitter and *wrong* coming from Jill. "Hell, right now, he could be you. You fit the description that I just gave. Blond, tall, strong, square jaw…is it any wonder that no one was able to find the guy?"

His hands tightened on her shoulders. "It *wasn't* your fault." He needed her to believe that.

"It wasn't until I started my criminal justice courses that I realized…eyewitness testimony is notoriously unreliable."

He didn't let her go. Her voice had softened. He should back away. But he didn't.

"Just with my work at the FBI, I've talked to so many witnesses…" She gave a sad shake of her head. "Witnesses who saw the *exact* same perp, but who described him in completely different ways. It's just…unreliable. *I* was unreliable. I could have described the man totally wrong. Even adult witnesses describe perps the wrong way…so, of course, a thirteen-year-old kid who'd been traumatized would make mistakes." She swallowed. "*I* made mistakes. To tell

you the honest truth, I can't even swear to what
I saw today. Maybe he wasn't blond. Maybe I
was just thinking of you. You had such a big
role in that day for me. Maybe *you* were all that
I could see."

She'd been all that he could see. The first person who'd looked at him as if he weren't trash,
as if he were someone who mattered. And then
he'd seen her get taken.

I can't lose her.

Those had been his thoughts that day. He remembered them perfectly.

I won't lose her.

"It's the human memory," she whispered.
"People think it's like a video recorder or something but it's not. The way people think…my
friend Samantha said it's more like putting puzzle pieces together. We have the bits and pieces
there, but sometimes our mind makes jumps to
fill in the rest for us. To close those gaps."

The wind caught a lock of her hair once more
and blew it over her cheek. His hand rose and
brushed back that hair, and then his fingers lingered on the silk of her skin. "It wasn't your
fault. Nothing was."

She sucked in a sharp breath and seemed to
become aware of just how close they were.

Aware that he was touching her.

I need to back away.

He started to ease away. His hand slid down her cheek and—

Jill caught his hand in hers. "It's because it hurts."

Hayden's eyes narrowed. "What hurts?" He *never* wanted Jill to feel pain. He would do anything necessary to see to it that she never suffered a single day of her life. Not—

"When you touch me, it hurts."

Her words pierced the heart she'd always owned.

"It makes me feel too much. *You* make me feel too much. You always did."

Was that good? Or bad?

"You make me want…" Jill said, giving a shake of her head. "You make me want things that I can't have."

Maybe they should be clear. She could have him anytime she wanted. Anytime, any way, any day. He was aroused for her right then. It was pretty much impossible for him to get close to Jill and *not* want her.

"That's dangerous," she continued, her voice husky. "*You're* dangerous to me."

No, he wasn't. She was the safest person in the world when he was near.

Her body brushed against his. It had been so long since he'd held her. Dreams weren't enough for him any longer. Memories could only get a man so far. She was close. He needed her.

A taste, just a taste to get him through…

"I never stopped wanting you," Hayden confessed. It was time to make sure there were no secrets between them.

Her lashes lowered. Such thick, dark lashes. The sunlight made her red hair gleam. "I tried to stop wanting you," she said.

He deserved that. Damn it. He sucked in a deep breath and made himself step back. "We shouldn't stay out too long. You always burned too easily." He should have brought her a hat. Or grabbed a beach umbrella. Her skin was so much paler than his own and—

Jill touched *him.* Her fingers curled around his wrist and Hayden stilled.

"I tried," she said, "but then I came face-to-face with you, and I realized the need is still there."

"Jill…"

"I'm not here to make the same mistakes. I'm here to get my life together. I'm here to end the past and to try and move on."

Was she saying he was the past?

"If I'd known you were here…" She licked her lips and didn't say another word.

"You wouldn't have come," Hayden finished. Damn, he hadn't realized just how much Jill hated him. He didn't want that. He *couldn't* deal with that. Not from her.

"No... I..." Her lashes lifted. "I would have been better prepared for you. I would have been able to hold myself back."

He didn't want her holding back.

"But maybe I'm making too much of this," Jill added, a faint furrow between her brows. "Maybe what I'm feeling...it's just left over from our past." Her gaze dropped to his mouth. "Why fear it...if I don't know what will happen?"

"Jill?"

Her hand fisted on his uniform shirt. "Kiss me."

Wait. Had she just said—

"Maybe I won't feel anything and I can let our past go."

"Don't count on it," Hayden growled. He bent his head and his lips took hers.

There was no uncertainty in his kiss, not with Jill. No getting-to-know-you hesitation. He knew her intimately, knew exactly what she liked and didn't like. All of those memories were burned into his mind.

She'd said people's memories were like puzzle pieces. His memories of her weren't. His memories of her were complete in heartbreaking detail because she'd been the one person who always mattered most to him.

Her lips parted beneath his. Hayden's tongue swept inside her mouth. She tasted so sweet, so good. He pulled her closer and kissed her deeper. He longed for so much more. A low moan built in her throat, a sexy sound that just made the desire knife through him. He was hard and aching for her.

But they were on a public beach.

People were around.

And she was...*running a test. Trying to see if she can walk away from me.*

His head slowly lifted. He stared down at her, saw the flush on her cheeks and the heat in her gaze. "Well?"

She let go of his uniform. "You always did know how to kiss. But then, you *were* the boy who gave me my very first kiss." She started to retreat.

Hayden caught her hand, held tight. *We are so past that not-touching part.*

"That first kiss was on this very beach." Another memory that had gotten him through hell. When his life had become a battle, when the missions had been at their darkest, he'd pulled out those memories.

"What do you want me to say?" Jill asked, her breath hitching. "What do you want—"

You. Always you. "Time has passed. We've changed. But the desire hasn't, Jill. It hasn't lessened." Hell, no. For him, it had only gotten stronger. Right then, he wanted her naked and under him on a bed. Or over him. That would work, too. Any way with Jill would work. "But the choice is yours." It always would be. "You want us to stay only partners, just working the cold case? Fine, we can do that." He'd need a whole lot of very, very icy showers. "But if you want more…" He exhaled. "Then I'll give you everything I have."

Her gaze searched his. What did she see, Hayden wondered, when Jill looked at him?

He knew what others had seen…

Troublemaker.

Son of a criminal.

Trash.

Then…after Jill…

Hero.

Fighter.

SEAL.

Now…sheriff. Peacekeeper.

But what was he to her? *An ex she wants to forget?* "So how did the experiment go?" Hayden asked her, his voice gruff. "Are we to be just partners or—"

"Wanting you was never a problem, Hayden."

His brows lifted at her hushed words.

"Loving you? That was where I made my mistake." She gave him a brisk nod. "I'm going back to my rental house for a few hours. I want to call some contacts at the FBI. You and I—we can talk more later." She turned and began to walk away.

"Talk about the case?" Hayden called out to her. "Or about us?"

She looked back at him. The wind tousled her hair, fanning it across her face. "Both."

HE WATCHED JILL as she headed toward her car. He hadn't been certain which vehicle was hers— there were too many rentals in town right then. But she went to the small sedan with quick, determined strides and he smiled.

But then she stopped. Her gaze lifted and she turned, scanning the street.

He wasn't outside so she didn't see him. He was nestled, all safe and snug, in the little deli. The perfect place to watch. Because the sun could be so incredibly bright, the thoughtful deli owners had gotten the windows tinted. Their customers could see out and enjoy the million-dollar beach view, but folks outside couldn't peer into the deli.

Jill couldn't see him.

He rolled back his shoulders and let his grin stretch. Did she feel him? Somehow sense him? He'd heard that folks could do that, could tell— instinctively—when they were prey.

Jill was prey. Very, very long overdue prey.

She lingered a moment longer, and her gaze slid back to the beach. The sheriff was there, walking slowly toward her. He'd seen them on the beach, too. Talking, like old friends.

Kissing, like lovers.

Hayden Black was an interfering SOB. He'd make sure the guy didn't get in his way again. After all…how could Hayden prevent a threat…

When he never saw it coming?

Chapter Four

The cemetery was so small. A white, picket fence provided the border for the property, and the graves that waited there…they were marked only by the small, fading headstones.

Jill stared down at the stone near her feet, the grave for Christy Anderson. *Beloved daughter. Gone, but never forgotten.*

No, Christy had certainly not been forgotten. Not by her family. *Not by me.* Even though Jill and Christy had never met, the girl was forever burned in Jill's memory.

Jill had read over the facts of Christy's abduction. She'd accessed the FBI database remotely, she'd searched NamUs, looking for other victims who matched her and Christy's age at the time they were taken in the National Missing and Unidentified Persons System. She'd tried to figure out just who the perp was, what darkness had driven him, what motivations had possessed him.

Christy had not been sexually abused when she'd been kidnapped. She hadn't been tortured. She'd just been killed, quickly, and then she'd been dumped on the beach.

Not dumped. Her body was carefully arranged. Her face was even covered with a blanket. Normally, that would have been a sign of remorse but...

"I'm not sure he regretted what he did, not to either of us," Jill whispered. The headstone was clean, gleaming in the fading light, while the other nearby markers were overgrown with weeds or covered in a layer of grime. Fresh daisies were near the grave. Someone was still looking after Christy. Someone was still taking care of her.

Never forgotten.

When she'd fled Georgia after that last case had gone to hell on her, Jill hadn't realized just why she was so desperate to return back to Hope. Her grandmother had died just after Jill's eighteenth birthday. She didn't have any family left, and she'd sold her grandmother's home to pay for her college tuition.

But...

I needed closure. I needed to stop running. I needed to stop feeling like I was still looking over my shoulder, waiting for the man who took me to appear again.

She could relate so well to the victims she faced each day on her job. Mostly because she *had* been them.

Jill rubbed her chilled arms and headed back to her car. She had another stop that she wanted to make, another visit that was overdue. This time, she wanted to see Christy's parents. She needed to talk to them about the last day of their daughter's life.

Jill was sure that little talk was going to be a nightmare and that was why she was planning to have Hayden accompany her. It wasn't as if the Andersons could slam their door shut on the local sheriff.

They *shouldn't* slam it shut on an FBI agent, either, but when it came to her, Theodore Anderson had never been the most...reasonable man.

Why did she get to live but I'm burying my daughter? Why? The echo of his scream still haunted her. He'd been in her grandmother's living room, and she'd been on the stairs, desperately trying to cover her ears so she wouldn't hear all the terrible things he was saying.

And she'd been wishing, so desperately, that

Hayden would appear. Bad things didn't happen when Hayden was close.

Until the day that Hayden *became* the bad thing in her life.

She headed for her rental car, she'd just taken a few steps when...

She heard the snap of a twig. Jill tensed and her gaze swung to the left, to the thick line of twisting pine trees and brush that covered the west side of the cemetery.

It wasn't uncommon for some wild animals to roam the area. Deer were often seen. Squirrels, rabbits—

Another twig snapped.

Every instinct Jill possessed told her that no squirrel was watching her. Her hand automatically went to her holster—only, she wasn't wearing the holster. She had her holster and her gun safely tucked away back in her room.

Her chin lifted. "Is someone there?"

No response. Not that she'd expected one. She glanced around the empty cemetery and felt a chill skirt down her spine. It wouldn't be the first time that a robber had waited near a cemetery, sure that a grieving—and distracted—family member would appear to be the perfect pickings. Time to make it clear—real clear—that she wasn't an easy target, gun or no gun. "I'm

FBI Agent Jillian West!" she yelled. "Identify yourself, now!"

Instead of someone stepping forward, she heard the fast thud of footsteps, running away. *Definitely not a squirrel.* Jill hesitated for only a second and then she gave chase. She rushed toward the brush and slipped into the woods. Twigs and branches tugged at her shirt and jeans, but she pushed past them, determined to follow those retreating footsteps. Determined to figure out just who had been watching her.

But then she heard the quick growl of an engine. She surged forward, pushing herself to run even faster. She broke through the trees, breath heaving, and saw the front of an SUV. Her gaze jerked toward the windshield, toward the man behind the wheel—

The SUV surged toward her. She could feel the heat from the engine and she rushed to the side, but the vehicle turned after her, nearly clipping her hip, and Jill flew forward. Her hands scraped over the ground, her knees hit the earth, and the SUV whipped past her as the driver shot down the narrow road.

Jill pushed herself up, gazing after the vehicle as it fled.

So much for her vacation. Her few days away were starting to prove to be as dangerous as her job with the FBI.

"SHERIFF BLACK?"

Hayden glanced up to see Finn standing nervously in his doorway.

"Just…just got a call in to the station, sir," Finn said, pulling at his collar. "From the FBI agent—"

Hayden surged to his feet. "Jill?" Wait, okay, he needed to tone down, way down. He cleared his throat. "Does Agent West need more case files?"

Finn's eyes were wide. "No. She…she was nearly hit near the Jamison Cemetery."

Hit?

"Some SUV almost ran her down. She got the tag and she wants us to figure out who—"

In an instant, he was around the desk. He grabbed Finn by the shoulders. "She's all right?" A dull thudding filled his ears. It took Hayden a moment to realize that was his heartbeat.

Finn nodded quickly. "She said she was fine! She's on her way here…just wanted us to get the tag number and she said she wanted to go with you to confront the bast—um, I mean the driver."

Hayden would be confronting the guy, all right. "Run the tag, *now*."

Finn scrambled to obey. Hayden checked his weapon and grabbed his coat. He didn't put up with crap like this in *his* town, and to think that the guy had nearly hit Jill. *His* Jill.

Oh, the hell, no.

Hayden marched out of his office. Finn was tapping frantically on the computer near his desk.

"Uh, Sheriff?"

Hayden narrowed his eyes on the deputy.

"It's a stolen vehicle. It was taken from a parking garage in Jacksonville a few days ago."

"Report the sighting," Hayden ordered.

"It's an older model," Finn added. "No GPS tracking."

Of course not, that would have made things too easy.

The bell jingled over the front entrance. Hayden spun around. Jill was there—

Her clothes were rumpled, dirty, and...was that *blood* on her cheek? He rushed to her and his hand lifted to touch her cheek. It was blood *and* a bruise. "I thought you weren't hit," he gritted out, fury burning in his blood.

She gave a little wince. "Trust me, it could have been about a thousand times worse. I managed to jump out of the way just in time."

Jump? Had she just said that she'd *jumped* out of the way? His fingers feathered over the bruise. "Come with me," he ordered. Then, not waiting for her to obey, he caught her wrist in his hand and tugged her toward his office. "The vehicle was stolen from Jacksonville." He shot a quick glare toward Finn. "Get an APB out for that SUV! I've got some drunk jerk running loose and—"

"I don't think he was drunk," Jill said quietly. "I think he deliberately tried to hit me."

Every muscle in his body tensed.

"Definitely get out that APB," Jill told Finn. "Maybe another one of the deputies will spot the guy so we can bring him in for questioning."

Hayden wasn't interested in questioning the suspect. He was interested in making the guy pay for hurting Jill. He was still new to the sheriff business. In his mind, he was a SEAL. Battle ready and focused.

Get the enemy.

He shut the door of his office, then gently pushed Jill into his desk chair. It was the plushest chair in the room. "Be right back."

She blinked, her brow furrowing, but he just hurried toward the bathroom—the sheriff's private bathroom was a nice perk of the office—and he came back a moment later with a warm cloth in his hand. Carefully, he wiped at the blood on her cheek. "It's not too bad," he said, but he was still furious. *She shouldn't be hurt at all.*

Jill lifted her hands. "These took the brunt of my fall."

He cursed. Then he was pulling her up and hauling her into the bathroom with him. He cleaned the wounds, bandaged them, all the while wanting to drive his fist into the face of the jerk who'd hurt her. "Tell me what happened," he demanded as he held her hands in his. "Everything."

The bathroom was small, a tight space, so they were intimately close. Jill rolled one shoulder in a shrug and said, "I was at the Jamison Cemetery—"

"Why," Hayden cut in.

She blinked at the sharpness of his voice.

He should try to dial back his rage, he got that but…this was Jill. Jill had always been his trigger. Something happened to her, and he freaked out.

That was just a general Hayden and Jill rule for life.

"Because I needed to pay my respects to Christy."

The guilt was there, sliding into her voice. "Jill…" Hayden began.

"Then I realized I wasn't alone."

His eyes narrowed.

"I heard someone in the woods right behind the cemetery. I called out to him and he ran."

His hand lifted to feather over her cheek. "So you followed him."

Her lips curled. "Of course. I'm an FBI agent. It's what I do."

You run into danger. Didn't he do the same thing? As a SEAL, he'd gotten addicted to the rush of adrenaline. To the thrill of the hunt. The blaze of battle.

"He had his vehicle stashed on Widow's Way."

He knew the old road that cut behind the cemetery. It had gotten the nickname because long ago, a widow who'd lost her husband at sea had traveled back and forth along that path every single day, desperate to see her husband.

"I tried to stop him but he…well, he had other plans." Her small nostrils flared. "The guy revved the engine and came right at me, even when I was trying to leap to safety. He *aimed* for me." Her gaze fell to her hands. Maybe he'd gone a little crazy with the bandages. "I was lucky to walk away with a few scrapes."

That driver wasn't going to be lucky when Hayden got hold of him.

"Probably some punk," she murmured, "looking to make some quick cash by robbing a visitor at the cemetery. And since you said the car was stolen."

"It was. A few days ago."

She nodded. "Obviously, we seem to have a

guy who likes to steal. He's probably long gone, but the APB might give us a shot at catching him before he slips from town."

Maybe. If the guy's plan was to vanish. "You said he was watching you?" Alarm bells were going off in his head.

"Yes, probably trying to decide if I was worth robbing. His mistake. Robbing an FBI agent is never a good plan."

No, it wasn't but...

He stared into her eyes. The greenest eyes he'd ever seen.

"I forgot about the gold," Jill whispered.

What?

"Hidden in the darkness..." Her head tilted as she stared into his eyes. "You have a warm gold in your eyes."

His heart slammed into his chest. He became aware of just how close they were, of how intimate their position was. His lower body brushed against hers, his hands were on her. He—

A fist pounded against his office door, making the already wobbly door rattle. "Sheriff!" Finn called. "Sheriff, we got him!"

Jill's eyes widened. Hayden spun away and rushed out of the bathroom and toward his office door. He yanked open the door and found Finn beaming at him.

"Got the car," Finn said. "Deputy Hollow just spotted it near the West End Beach."

THE SUV WAS at the West End, all right, but there was no sign of the driver. Hayden put his hands on his hips as he surveyed the scene.

"Guess the guy up in Jacksonville will be real glad to get his ride back, huh?" Deputy Wendy Hollow murmured, her lips curling. The sun had set and the only light on them came from the bright moon over their heads. The West End Beach was the most remote beach in the area. Locals were the only ones who ever came down there because most of the tourists didn't even know it existed, a deliberate secret.

For the SUV to be abandoned there...

"The driver had to go someplace," Hayden said. He looked around, but there was no sign of another civilian vehicle, just Deputy Hollow's patrol car and his vehicle—Hayden had gotten Jill to drive over with him. "Not like the guy just vanished into thin air."

"We can check the car for prints," Jill said as she stood near him. "The suspect probably left plenty of evidence behind. He was looking to ditch the car and make a break for it. Our run-in at the cemetery probably scared him."

Hayden still wasn't so sure of that fact. During the past ten years, he'd learned to never ignore his instincts. When he was in the field, they always warned him when danger was coming. Right then, his instincts were screaming at him.

Jill was being watched at the cemetery. Now the vehicle her watcher used is abandoned and the driver is long gone. He turned toward her. "I think you should have protection tonight."

She laughed.

He didn't. "I'm serious, Jill. This scene..." He waved his hand. "It's not right. It's...off... and you know it."

"I'm an FBI agent, I think I can manage to look after myself tonight." She turned away.

He followed right on her heels. Hayden reached out and curled his hand around her shoulder.

She looked back at him, frowning. "Hayden..."

"Even FBI agents need protection."

"Look, I get that things are personal between us, but I just have a few scratches. It wasn't anything life threatening."

"He tried to run you down!"

"Because he panicked." She looked over his shoulder, gazing at the abandoned SUV. "Prints are going to turn up in there. You'll find the guy, I have no doubt. The streets of Hope will be safe again."

But would *she* be safe?

Jill didn't seem worried.

Hayden sure as hell was. Because…
This is you, Jill. And I will always protect you.

HE'D MADE A mistake at the cemetery. He should
have stayed farther back. Should have kept his
distance.

But he'd wanted to get closer.

She'd looked so sad as she stood there, staring
at the grave. She'd seemed such perfect prey. All
alone. Prime for the taking. But…

Then he'd heard her voice, barking with authority, reminding him that she wasn't the girl
he'd known before. She was an FBI agent now
and he hadn't been able to tell if she was armed.

If she'd had her gun…if she'd shot at him…

I don't want to die. That was his truth. He
wasn't anywhere near ready to die.

So he'd run. Fast. Hard. He'd fled and when
she'd come rushing out of the woods, well,
he'd taken that opportunity to end her. But he'd
missed. She'd seen his car, and he'd had to dump
it.

No big deal. He'd taken the vehicle when he'd
been in Jacksonville. Taken it because…

*Some habits die hard. I always liked to keep
a throwaway vehicle close, in case I find a special girl.*

Jill West was a very special girl to him. Very

special, indeed. The one that got away. The one
that had changed so much for him.

He glanced up at her beachfront cabin. It was
dark now because she was gone. Probably out
hunting for him. *Never expected that I'd be waiting at home for you, did you, Jillian?* But here
he was...

And he'd stay in the shadows. He'd wait until
she came back. And then the real fun would
begin. Because he'd carefully considered the situation with her. He didn't want to launch an attack straight at her, no, with her FBI training,
that wasn't a fight he wanted.

He'd take the easy way. The better way.

He'd attack Jill when she was vulnerable. And
the most vulnerable time for a woman? For *anyone*?

That would be during sleep. When Jill slipped
away in her dreams, he'd go to her. He'd wait
and bide his time and he'd watch. But the moment her guard was lowered, he would be there.

*And, Jill, you will pay for everything that you
took away from me.*

Chapter Five

Her little rental cabin was dark when Jill pulled into the narrow drive. She'd stayed at the scene with Hayden, she'd helped search the area, but the driver had been long gone. Maybe he'd slipped away on some of the trails in the area. Maybe he'd had another ride waiting.

The maybes hadn't mattered. One fact was clear—he was gone, and it was highly doubtful they'd find the guy that night.

Hayden had taken her back to the station. She'd gotten her car, refused his protection one more time, and she'd pretended not to see the frustration that had filled his gaze. Spending the night with Hayden *wasn't* a good idea. She knew that.

Her feelings for him were too raw. When he'd been bandaging her hands in that little bathroom, she'd stared at him and just ached.

Too many memories were between them. Too much desire still remained.

When she climbed up the long flight of wooden steps that led to her cabin, Jill felt a bone-deep weariness. She unlocked the door. The wind blew off the ocean, bringing her the salty scent on the breeze. Jill looked back at that water. The waves gleamed beneath the moonlight. The water had always soothed her, even when she'd been at her absolute worst.

The water…and Hayden. Her two constants in life.

Jill turned away from the ocean. She shut the door behind her and flipped the lock. There was no security system at the cabin, so she took a few moments to do a quick search and to double-check all of the locks on the windows and on the screen door that slipped away from the kitchen and led back to the big front deck. Side effect of the job…being hypervigilant. She'd seen too many horror stories, firsthand.

Jill headed into her bedroom. When she passed the TV, the floor gave a low groan. She couldn't help but tense at the sound. *This day has been too long.* Now she was nearly jumping at—quite literally—nothing. She'd shower and crash into bed. And maybe, if she was lucky, she wouldn't dream about two bright headlights coming toward her. She wouldn't remember the heat of the engine as it growled beside her.

If she was lucky.

HAYDEN SLOWED HIS vehicle as he slowly drove by Jill's cabin. One light glowed in her cabin. Jill was still awake. She'd refused his multiple offers of protection.

And he got it, he really did. She could take care of herself. Hell, yes, he'd read the stories about her work. Jill had often been in the headlines, particularly when she worked high-profile cases. She'd taken down some of the worst scum out there. He knew she was smart, tough and absolutely deadly with her gun but…

But this is Jill. If something happens to her, I worry I'll lose my damn sanity.

His hands tightened on the steering wheel.

And, as if on cue, the light in her cabin turned off.

Jill was in, safe and sound, for the night. Time for him to get the hell out of there. He accelerated but… Hayden couldn't help glancing back in his rearview mirror.

This is Jill. If something happens to her…

WAKEFULNESS CAME IN a sudden rush. One instant, Jill had been completely asleep, lost to her dreams, but in the next, her eyes were wide-open and a cold chill iced her blood.

She didn't move in that bed. Her heart galloped in her chest. She had an animal awareness crawling over her—*something is wrong*. Something had woken her, but she didn't know what. She didn't move so much as a finger as she tried to figure out what had brought her awake with such a sharpness.

Then…she heard the scraping. A small, faint sound. And…

She knew what caused that sound. When she'd opened the sliding glass door before—the door that led from the kitchen to the front deck, the screen had scraped when the door slid open. Wind and time had damaged the screen and when the door slid open a few inches, the screen scraped.

But she'd checked that door before bed. She *remembered* checking the lock. The door had been closed. There was no reason for it to scrape now.

Unless someone is out there.

Her fingers slowly moved toward the pillow on the other side of her bed. Before she'd gone to bed, she'd put her weapon there, wanting it to be close just in case. Her fingers touched the gun.

And she heard a groan.

This time, the sound was a little bit louder. As

if the groan had come from the den. And again, she knew that sound…when she'd walked in front of the TV out there, the floor had groaned beneath her feet. There was a weak spot of wood. A spot that creaked when someone stepped on it.

Someone is out there. Someone is coming closer.

She'd shut her bedroom door. Locked it but…

Did she hear the soft click of that lock turning? Was it her imagination?

Jill took a deep breath. Her index finger slid off the safety of her gun. Her eyes had adjusted to the darkness and she was staring straight at her door.

It was opening.

"Freeze!" Jill yelled. "Freeze or I will shoot."

The door stilled. Each breath she took seemed far too loud.

Then…

Laughter. Cold. Mocking laughter. "You think you're the only one with a gun, Agent West?"

Oh, damn.

"You should have left Christy Anderson alone." The snarled words came from her doorway.

She dived for the side of the bed even as the thunder of a gunshot filled the room. *You missed!* She stayed low but Jill lifted up just enough to fire back.

But he was running. She could hear the thunder of her intruder's footsteps. Jill didn't hesitate. She jumped to her feet and rushed after him. "Stop!" she yelled.

He didn't. He *did* fire wildly back at her and Jill had to duck when the bullet sank into the wood a few inches away from her. The screen door scraped and his footsteps thudded over the wooden steps outside.

She should call for backup. Jill knew it, but she also knew if she stopped long enough to call the sheriff's office, her intruder would be long gone.

So she clutched her gun and she ran after him. When she got on the long line of wooden steps that led down to the beach, she saw him fleeing beneath the light of the moon. A man, tall, with broad shoulders. He was moving fast, too fast. Sand kicked up around his feet.

"Stop!" Jill yelled.

But he didn't.

And neither did she.

So HE WAS OBSESSED. Hayden knew he had a problem. When it came to Jill, it was a very, very long-standing problem.

It was the middle of the night and he couldn't sleep. And he was driving by her cabin again because he obviously had issues.

But when his headlights cut across the beach, he caught a glimpse of a woman running—a woman wearing a T-shirt and shorts.

A woman with a gun clutched in her hand.

Jill.

He slammed on the brakes. Hayden grabbed his own gun from the glove box and took off after her. His heart pounded a double-time rhythm in his chest. Jill was zigzagging in front of him, rushing frantically down the beach and kicking up sand in her wake. The moonlight shone down on her and—

And on the jerk she's chasing.

Because Hayden could see him. A dark, shadowy form about twenty feet in front of Jill. A shadow that was whirling back around and lifting his gun. *Firing.*

"Jill!" Hayden bellowed.

But she'd already ducked. The gunfire blasted and Hayden *thought* it had missed her. He prayed it had. The guy seemed to be shooting wildly now, panicking. Whoever the hell that man was, he'd better be afraid.

This was Hayden's town.

He drove himself faster, faster, determined to catch the jerk up ahead. But the man had rushed off the beach, heading toward another dark cabin. A moment later, the growl of an engine reached Hayden's ears.

He saw a motorcycle hurtle from beneath that cabin. The motorcycle rushed into the darkness, flying away with its light off and the driver not even looking back.

Jill lifted her gun and aimed after him. Then she shook her head and Hayden heard her curse.

He ran to her, grabbed her arm and swung her toward him. "Jill!" His gaze flew frantically over her, but he didn't see any injures. "Baby, are you okay?"

"No, I'm not." She jerked away from him. "He got away!" She still had her gun gripped in her hand. "Should have known he had a getaway vehicle close by." Jill whirled on her heel—her bare heel because he realized she was shoeless—and glared into the night.

Hayden yanked out his phone. "Not gone yet." He connected with the sheriff's office. He started barking orders to Dispatch even as he grabbed Jill's arm. They ran back toward his vehicle and he pushed her into the passenger's side. "We're tailing the suspect now," Hayden said into his phone. "Get backup out here…this guy is armed and dangerous and I'm not having him run wild over *my* town."

He threw the SUV into reverse. The wheels squealed as he gave chase. "Tell me what in the hell happened."

Jill flattened her palm against the dashboard.

"I woke up…and I heard him coming into the cabin."

What?

"He came to my bedroom."

The SOB was going to pay.

"I told him to stop, that I had a gun."

His foot had rammed the accelerator all the way to the floorboard.

"And he told me that he did, too. Then he fired."

His hands had fisted around the steering wheel. "You're not hurt." He needed to hear her say those words again.

"I'm not." She leaned forward. "I don't see him." Frustration hummed in her words.

He didn't see the guy, either. The road they were on was long and twisting, and it didn't connect with the highway for another six miles. He was hoping one of his deputies would cut off that highway entrance—that had been his order. The deputy would block the guy from the front and Hayden would get the guy from the back.

Provided, of course, that the guy on the motorcycle didn't go off road. If he did, if he slipped onto any of the trails around there…

We lose him.

HE HAD TO get off the bike. He risked a quick glance behind him and saw the glare of two headlights. He had a lead, a damn good one, but Jill would make sure everyone in Hope was looking for a man on a motorcycle. She'd get an APB out on him, and he'd be hunted.

I have to ditch this thing.

Where and when…hell, that was the question. It was dark, so that worked to his advantage. If he cut across the sand, his tracks wouldn't be spotted until the sun was up.

He could go through the woods. Follow a trail. Ditch the bike there or…

The scent of the ocean teased him.

Or he could try a different escape path.

He drove off the road. The bike spit up sand as the wheels churned. The beach was deserted, as it freakin' well should have been at that time of the night. He ditched the bike, tucked his gun into the back of his jeans and his gloved fingers fisted as he ran right toward the surf.

Jill could get every deputy in the area to search the roads for him, but he wasn't escaping via land.

He was heading for the water. The last place they'd expect to look. *Search the roads all night. Search every trail. I won't be there.*

The water lapped at his feet.

Good thing he was a strong swimmer.

THEY REACHED THE highway and Hayden braked when he saw the flash of patrol lights. Deputy

Hollow stood beside her car, her hand on her holster. Hayden jumped out and ran toward her, aware that Jill was following close beside him. "Tell me you saw the guy," he said.

But Wendy shook her head. "Sorry...no one has come past me."

He whirled back around and stared at the darkness behind him.

"He diverted," Jill said. "He wanted to stay off the main road. He was planning this from the beginning, that's why he was on a motorcycle. Easier for him to slip into the woods."

To vanish.

"Get more units out here," Hayden ordered. "I want to search every trail. This guy is armed, he's been shooting, and I want him taken down."

Wendy nodded quickly and she slid into her car as she contacted Dispatch. Jill started to rush by Hayden, but he caught her arm. "What are you doing?"

"I'm going to help search. When backup arrives, we can coordinate into teams to divide the area and—"

"You don't even have shoes on your feet!" He pulled her closer. His voice dropped as he said, "I told you that you were in danger."

He heard the stutter of her breath. "Hayden, I'm fine."

"He shot at you." And that shook him, straight

to his core. "I should have been with you. I should have—"

"We've covered this before." Now her voice was nearly a whisper. "How many times do I have to tell you, you can't protect me twenty-four hours a day?"

It was an old argument between them. Actually, it was one of the things that had driven them apart. When it came to Jill, he held on too tight.

He wanted too much.

Hayden glanced down at his hands. *Too tight.* He forced himself to let her go.

"He said something else."

Hayden shook his head, not following her.

"Before he fired at me, in my bedroom, he said...he said I should have left Christy Anderson alone."

Every muscle in his body locked down.

"I was at Christy's grave earlier...so I think... it must be the same man from the cemetery," Jill continued, her voice strained. "I thought he was there to rob me, but..."

"He came tonight to kill you." Brutal words, but if the man had broken into her home with a gun... Hayden's control snapped. He wrapped his hands around her shoulders again and yanked her close. *"I should have been there."*

"Hayden..."

"You just came back. And I could have lost

you already." Hell, no. *No.* This wasn't happening. He wouldn't let it happen. "We're finding that sicko, and I'm going to make sure that he *never* hurts you again."

THE TRACKS WERE found near dawn, when the streaks of light crept across the sky and showed where the motorcycle had slipped off the road. The guy had been good, Jill would give him that much. He'd hidden the bike behind the dunes to make it harder to spot. The shifting sands had already blown over part of the line that had been left by the motorcycle's tires.

He must have walked away after he'd ditched the bike, but the sand was perfectly smooth as it led to the water. No sign of his footprints.

He knew those would be gone by dawn.

They'd been searching the area all night. Hayden had made sure she got shoes, and she'd made sure she was involved in the hunt. But despite their efforts, they hadn't come across the intruder. Maybe that was because he hadn't been on land. Her eyes narrowed as she stared at those waves.

Hayden was at her side, silent, angry. She could feel the frustration rolling off him.

"This man knows the town," Jill said. Not just the town...the whole area. He knew the private beaches, he knew the back roads. He knew the water.

They weren't looking for some drifter.

"The fact that he mentioned Christy, that he came for me…" Jill turned to stare at Hayden. "I think—"

"We're going to pay a visit to the Anderson family," he said.

Her stomach tightened. A trip to visit the Andersons had been on her agenda even before this madness had started. Christy's father had been so angry with her years ago, and when she'd been a teen and their paths had crossed in town, he'd always stared at her with such a cold, hard gaze.

She knew he hated her.

But…

Was he enraged enough to have come after her with a gun?

Chapter Six

The Andersons still lived at 1509 Sea Breeze Way. Jill climbed out of Hayden's car—his patrol car, not his SUV, he'd switched vehicles since he was on official business—and she slammed the door shut as she stared up at the house. It was clean, perfectly tidy with neatly trimmed hedges and a well-swept sidewalk. The house appeared to have been freshly painted white, and the shutters were a light blue to match the ocean.

From the outside, it looked like such a happy home. Such a normal place.

She knew just how deceiving appearances could truly be. She'd walked up to too many houses—ordinary houses just like the one at 1509 Sea Breeze Way—and found monsters living inside.

"Jill?"

She shook her head and glanced over at Hayden. He was wearing his sheriff's uniform.

The badge shone in the light. They'd been up for most of the night and a line of dark stubble coated his jaw. He looked strong and…sexy.

And she really shouldn't be noticing that fact right then. She had enough to deal with as it was.

"You okay?" He moved to her side. His head cocked as he studied her. "For a minute there, I could have sworn that you were a million miles away."

Because she had been. "Sometimes, houses look perfect. Lives look perfect." She shook her head. "But they aren't."

He glanced back at the Andersons' house.

"In the case file, there were only minimal notes about her family. Peek never interrogated the father or mother. He just got general details from them about Christy, what she was wearing, what she'd done right before her disappearance…" Her words trailed away, and Jill pressed her hands to the top of her thighs. She wore dress pants and a crisp white shirt…what Jill thought of as her FBI gear. A light coat hid her holster. When working a case, it was standard protocol for agents to dress a certain way, and she'd gotten into the habit of almost arming herself with the clothing.

"You think they should have been interrogated?"

A curtain moved inside of the house. Someone was watching them. "Every case that CARD works…we *always* question the family." They were the starting point. And often, they were the very first suspects. "The first time I worked a case as an official CARD team member, I was looking for an eight-year-old boy who'd gone missing from his house in Birmingham, Alabama. His mother said that someone had come in during the night and taken him. There were signs of a struggle and his bedroom window was found open." Her hand lifted and, this time, her fingers pressed to her heart. It had started to ache. "Thirty minutes after we started to interview the mom, we noticed the inconsistencies in her story."

"Hell."

She pressed harder against her chest. "We found his body in the shed."

He caught her hand. Pulled her close. "I'm so sorry, Jill."

"Monsters," she whispered, blinking away the tears. "They're everywhere. I thought I'd join the FBI and save people, but that isn't happening, and I don't know what I—" She broke off because the door to 1509 Sea Breeze Way had just opened. "This isn't the right time," she said, her voice as soft as the wind blowing against them. "They're watching."

Hayden slowly turned toward the house. He

moved so that his body was in front of hers, a deliberate position, she knew. A protective one. *Some things never change.* Jill swiped her hands over her cheeks, but the skin was dry. She hadn't let the tears fall.

She couldn't remember the last time they'd fallen.

I didn't cry when we lost Jessica. I stared at the ambulance with dry eyes. I didn't cry when I talked to her family. I was just...too numb.

That was how she felt most days. Numb.

But...she didn't feel numb when Hayden was near her.

"You shouldn't be sheriff." The words were angry as they spewed from the man standing in that doorway.

Hayden gave a grim nod. "Hello, Mr. Anderson. Nice to see you, too."

A grunt came from Theodore Anderson.

Jill slipped to Hayden's side so that she could study the other man. Theodore Anderson was tall, still fit, but his blond hair had thinned. He was dressed in faded jeans and a loose sweatshirt. The lines on his face were deep, and his lips were pulled down in a frown as he gazed at Hayden.

"You aren't qualified for the job. I don't care what kind of war hero crap you pulled overseas," Theodore snapped. "Your father was a bum, a criminal who deserved exactly what he got, and you have no place—"

Hayden lifted his hand, stopping the guy's snarled words. "I *am* the sheriff here, and it would be wise to speak to me with a little more respect."

Theodore's face flashed red.

"I know you haven't had an easy time of things," Hayden said, voice curt, "but you need to calm yourself down, right now."

Theodore's chin jerked up. "What do you want?"

Hayden glanced at Jill, then he looked back at Theodore. "We have some questions for you."

"Questions? About what?" But Theodore's gaze had slid to Jill and he stared at her suspiciously. She didn't see recognition in his stare, not yet, his eyes were narrowed as they locked on her face.

"This FBI agent is following up on Christy's disappearance," Hayden said.

He hadn't told Theodore her name. Why? Did he think he was protecting her?

She wasn't going to hide. Jill cleared her throat and stepped forward. "I'm FBI Agent Jillian West."

And there it was. The recognition, flooding his face and turning his eyes cold and angry in a flash. His jaw locked and he glared at her with pure hate in his eyes. "Get *off* my property."

"Mr. Anderson, I'm investigating Christy's disappearance." The fact that the joker who'd taken a shot at her had mentioned Christy, well, that had just made her more determined than ever to find out the truth. "I'd like to ask you some questions about her last day with you."

"Why the hell are you digging that up now? Christy is gone!" His eyes glittered. "Dead and buried in the Jamison Cemetery."

"Yes, about that," Hayden murmured as he cocked his head and studied the other man. "When was the last time you were at that cemetery?"

"I go every week," Theodore fired back. "I make sure my daughter's grave is clean. That she is taken care of. I didn't take care of her while she was alive, but I will damn well do it while she's dead."

He doesn't just blame me for Christy's death. He blames himself, too. Jill could see that.

"And the date of your last visit was...?" Hayden asked.

"Yesterday. I go every Saturday, okay?"

So he'd just admitted to being there, the same day that someone had been watching her. *The same day someone tried to run me down.*

"Did you happen to see anyone while you were there?" Hayden's voice was mild.

"Why in the hell are you asking that?" Theodore shook his head. "No, I didn't see anyone. It was just me, got it? I swept her grave off, I put down fresh flowers and I left." Theodore took an aggressive step toward them. "FBI *special* agent," he said, lips twisting in distaste. "You think I haven't heard the stories about you, too? You go out there, you get your name in the papers and you—"

"And I try to bring home the children who were taken." She kept her voice calm with an effort. "I try to find children like Christy who were stolen from their families and I try to bring them back home, safe and sound so that their parents don't have to go and visit cemeteries every single week."

For an instant, his face crumpled.

"I'm in Hope for a little while, and I wanted to see if I could use my resources to bring closure to Christy's case."

His lips were trembling.

"I want to find the man who hurt her. I know you blame me for what happened to her—"

He turned away from Jill. "Hard to look at you," he rasped.

"Mr. Anderson—"

"Hard to look at you…because Christy would've been your age. I see you and I see everything I lost." He still wasn't looking at her. Maybe he couldn't, not any longer. "I see you… and I'm always reminded you came home, and she didn't."

His grief was heavy in the air.

His shoulders hunched. "My wife…she left me a few years back. Said she couldn't take it any longer. No more living with Christy's ghost, the pain was too much for her. She moved up to Washington. Took my son with her but he came back at least. Kurt's staying with me now. He's all I have left."

"I want to find her killer," Jill told him. "But I need your help."

Theodore still wasn't looking at her. "Peek said the guy was a drifter. In town probably just for the weekend. Took you, but you got away. So he took my Christy. Killed her and was long gone even before we found the body."

"That is one option." Jill shared a long glance with Hayden. "But there are others." Especially in light of her late-night visitor.

Theodore turned to frown at her. "What do you think happened?"

"I don't think a man like this would just kill one girl and never target anyone else again."

He backed up a step. His gaze fell.

"He took me, I got away, so he immediately acted again." Her lips pressed together. "I think it's fair to say he could have other victims out there, too. Back when he killed Christy, it was harder for authorities to connect the dots, especially when killers went across state lines or when they chose victims who had different ages or sexes. It was harder to piece together profiles because all of the information was so scattered."

Theodore swiped his hand over his face. She noticed that his fingers trembled.

"I want to help Christy. That's why I need to talk to you about the day she went missing. I want to know if you saw anything or anyone who was suspicious. If Christy mentioned *anyone* watching her. If she—"

"She was a good girl. She went to softball practice first thing that morning. She rode away on her bike." He glanced toward the garage. "And she never came back home. Her bike…it was found on the side of the road. Just left behind and she was gone. No one saw anything." His chin trembled as his stare jerked back to Hayden. "There was no one to race after my girl."

Hayden's hands had fisted.

"She died alone and that fact haunts me every single day of my life. I can hear her, in my mind." He tapped his temple. "I think she probably cried for me. And I wasn't there. I couldn't help her... *I wasn't there.*"

"Mr. Anderson—" Jill began.

He shook his head. "I need you to leave. I don't... I just can't talk to you any more now." His voice wasn't angry. He just suddenly seemed very, very tired.

She *needed* his help but she couldn't force his cooperation. Jill pulled a discrete white card from her pocket. She stepped toward him and held out the card. "This is my contact information. If you change your mind, please call me."

His gaze lingered on the card, but he made no move to take it.

"With or without your cooperation, I plan to continue my investigation." Because obviously, there was a lot for her to learn in that town. She didn't lower her hand. She kept that card extended.

The seconds ticked by. Then his hand reached up and he snatched the card from her. He turned, his movements angry and jerky and—he stilled. "I know you were there that day."

Jill looked back at Hayden. He was staring at Theodore Anderson, with his eyes narrowed and his face locked in tight lines.

"When I came to your grandmother's house, drunk, desperate, I know you were there." His hand had curled tightly around her card, crumpling it.

A car's engine rumbled and Jill saw a big, sleek vehicle pull to a stop near Hayden's patrol car. A tall man with sandy-blond hair and wide shoulders jumped from the fancy car. "Dad?" The man's voice rose. "Dad, what's happening? What's wrong?"

But Theodore didn't look at the man who was rushing toward him. "When I came to that house, I said you should have died in her place."

She didn't let herself flinch.

"It was wrong, and I knew it…"

"Dad?"

Jill knew the man staring at them in confusion was Christy's older brother, Kurt. He'd been in class with Hayden. A quiet, intense boy with bright blue eyes.

"What's happening here?" Kurt demanded once more.

"It's still wrong," Theodore whispered. "But I still… I feel the same way. I wish you were in the ground and my Christy was here with me." Then he shuffled up the steps that led back to his house.

Her heart was squeezing in her chest.

Kurt moved to follow his father, and then he stopped, glaring at Hayden. "Okay, Hayden, tell me what is going on."

Jill swallowed. "We're investigating Christy's death."

His eyes sharpened on her. "Jill?" Shock deepened his voice.

She gave him a tight smile. "Hello, Kurt. It's been a long time." As if following his father's lead, he'd never spoken to her much in school. In fact, he'd seemed to take deliberate pains to avoid her.

His focus jumped between her and Hayden. "You brought *her* to see my dad? 'Cause you thought that was a good idea?" His skepticism was clear.

"It was *my* idea," Jill said before Hayden could answer. "I wanted to talk to Mr. Anderson about the day Christy disappeared."

Kurt raked his hand through his hair. "Right. Let's just rub salt in that wound, why don't we?" He shook his head. "Christy is buried. Just let her rest in peace."

She was stunned by that answer. "Don't you *want* to find her killer?"

"My father is one year and seven months sober. *One year. Seven months.* I just got him back. I didn't plan on losing everyone in my family, but that's what happened when Christy was found on that beach. My whole world splintered apart." He heaved out a breath. "So just let it all go, got it? The past is dead and buried. Leave Christy alone."

You should have left Christy Anderson alone.

A chill skated down her spine.

Kurt hurried up the steps and followed his father inside of the house. She turned back to Hayden. His jaw had locked.

"They're not going to help, Jill," he said softly.

He was right but... "That doesn't mean I'm going to stop."

His lips hitched into that little half smile of his. The smile that always made her feel a bit warmer. "No, I didn't think that you would."

"ARE THEY GONE?" Theodore Anderson demanded.

Kurt peered through the window. He'd eased the curtains back just a bit so he could see outside. "They're getting into the patrol car now." Hayden had opened the passenger side door for Jill, and when she passed the sheriff, he noticed the guy's hand lingered just a moment on her arm.

Still as obsessed with her as ever. Everyone had known that truth in school. Hayden Black loved Jill West. The two had been inseparable. Until Hayden walked away from Jill. Most folks still didn't even know he'd left her. But Hayden had gone off to be all he could be, and Jill...

FBI special agent Jill West. "She just wants to help," he said, feeling sad for her. For them all.

"We don't need her help. Christy is at peace now. It's time to move the hell on."

Hayden was walking around the car, but his gaze lifted and, just for a moment, his stare seemed to lock on Kurt.

Kurt let go of the curtain and stepped back.

"Christy is dead and buried," his father muttered. "She deserves her peace. She doesn't need some FBI agent picking around at her...hell, this isn't some TV show. No one's going to go digging up my girl—"

Kurt's eyes widened as he spun to face his dad. "Is that what she wanted to do?"

His father was pacing, his movements tight and angry. "That's what they do on TV! They exhume the bodies, look for evidence and run all their tests."

Look for evidence. Kurt swallowed. "You don't want that to happen?"

Tears glittered in his father's eyes. "She's at peace now. I want her to stay that way. And I—I don't want to bury her again." His dad's face crumpled. "I need a drink."

"No," Kurt snapped out the denial. "That's the last thing you need." He closed the distance between them and put his hand on his dad's shoulder. "I'll take care of Jill West, okay?

Don't worry about her. Christy can have her peace. I'll make sure of it."

JILL WAS DEAD on her feet. Not that she'd ever admit it, Hayden realized, but he could see the weariness pulling at her.

He eased his patrol car to a stop next to her cabin. The sun was dipping low over the ocean, striking the waves a dark red. It had been one hell of a day. They'd spent hours searching for her intruder, going over crime scene details, getting the motorcycle checked for prints.

Only there hadn't been any.

Just as there hadn't been any prints left on the stolen SUV that had been abandoned on the West End.

"Thanks for the ride back," Jill murmured.

Oh, she thought he'd just given her a ride? That was cute. Sweet.

She climbed from the car and her fingers moved in a little wave. "Guess we'll pick up tomorrow?"

Um, no.

"Good night." She slammed the door shut and headed for her cabin.

The same cabin some creep had broken into the night before. The same place that had meager locks and far too easy access.

He slid out of the vehicle and followed behind her.

Jill stopped and glanced over her shoulder. "Is
there a problem?"

A very big one. "How long do you think it
will take you to get your things?"

Her eyes widened. "My...things?"

"Yes, you know...fresh clothes. Your laptop,
any other items that you feel you can't live without tonight."

"Why would I need my things?" She put her
hands on her hips and faced him.

He stalked closer to her. All day long, he'd
been walking on a tightrope. That rope was way
too close to snapping. *He came after Jill. He'd
shot at her.* "You aren't staying here alone tonight."

Her eyes widened. "Uh, excuse me?"

"That intruder—"

"I think I did a pretty good job of defending
myself."

She didn't get it. "Do you want me to stay
sane?"

Her brow furrowed. "That would probably be
a good plan."

He thought so, too. Hayden nodded. "Then
you're staying with me tonight. I'll have a deputy keep watch on your place."

She crossed her arms over her chest. "Did you just tell me I was staying at your place?"

"I did." He inclined his head toward her.

"I'm not afraid, Hayden. If he comes back, I'll be ready for him. I'll be—"

"I know you're not scared." He got that. What she didn't get... "I am."

She laughed. "Right, the big, bad navy SEAL is afraid. You're—"

"Absolutely terrified that something will happen to you."

Her smile slipped away. His hand rose and his fingers slid into the thickness of her hair as he tilted her head back and stared into her eyes. "You just don't get that, do you, Jill? You don't see how important you are to me."

"So important that you walked away." There was pain in her words. Pain that he *hated*.

"I wasn't going to stand in your way. I cared about you too much for that."

Her lips parted.

"What was the *one* thing you always wanted to do?" Hayden pushed.

She licked her lips. "Join the FBI."

He nodded. "And you did. You're a great agent, I know that. I also know that you had to leave Hope to follow that dream." His thumb brushed over her cheek. "So you had to leave me."

Her eyes seemed to flash at him. "I didn't

leave you. You're the one who walked away from *me*. The one who wanted adventure. The world…because I wasn't enough."

No, that wasn't what he'd thought. Not ever. "You were always enough." Then, because he wouldn't lie to her, Hayden confessed. "*I* wasn't."

Everyone in town had known that truth. Why hadn't she?

"Hayden…"

"You're the FBI agent," he murmured. "But I'm the town sheriff. Right now, my authority trumps yours. You're the crime victim in this case, not the investigator." He couldn't stop touching her. "So you have two choices. One, you come with me. You stay the night at my house."

"That's an interesting take on protective custody," she said, voice wry.

Oh, he'd make sure she was protected plenty. "Option two, we both stay at your cabin tonight." And if her late-night visitor came back, they'd both be ready.

"Option three," Jill added, "I stay by myself and you get back in your patrol car."

"It's not happening. You were nearly killed *twice* in the past twenty-four hours. My job is to keep the people of my town safe. *You're* one of those people, FBI badge or not. So you're either coming with me or I'll be bunking down with you."

He waited for more arguments. He waited…

"You know, when you're this close and when you touch like that… I keep expecting you to kiss me."

Okay, he hadn't expected *that* response. His heartbeat kicked up. "Do you *want* me to kiss you?"

"That's the problem, Hayden. I'm not sure what I want from you. Sometimes, I want you as far away from me as you can get."

Hell.

"And other times…" Her voice had gone so soft. "I feel like you're the one person in the world I need to hold close. Hold you close and tight."

And never let go. Because that was the way he felt about her. He wanted to grab Jill and hold her close, keep her safe and never, ever let her go again.

"You know what's better than one FBI agent waiting for a perp to attack?" Jill asked.

She was losing him. He wanted to get back to talking about her needing him close.

"An FBI agent *and* a sheriff waiting…that's what is better. So I'll take option two. You can bunk down on the couch." She stepped back.

His hand fell to his side.

"*Just* the couch, Hayden. I'm not offering anything else."

If only she was. She marched toward the cabin.

"Jill!" Hayden called.

She kept walking.

He smiled after her. "When you figure out what it is that you want from me, just let me know." *Hold you close. Never let go.* "After all, I'll be on your couch, so you just come out and tell me."

She gave a little snarl. His smile stretched. Maybe she didn't see it, but he was making progress with her. Real progress.

They just might have a real chance together.

If they could just put the past to rest.

Chapter Seven

"Do you still have nightmares?"

Hayden's quiet question caught Jill off guard. She'd just pulled an extra blanket from the hall closet, and she looked toward him, grasping that blanket close to her body.

"You used to have them a lot," he noted. "I was...just curious."

She hurried across the room and put the blanket on the sofa, right next to the extra pillows she'd already gotten out for him. "Worried I'll wake you up with my screams?" Jill backed away from the couch and turned—only to find him right in her path.

"No, that's not what I'm worried about. I'm worried about *you*."

Her breath whispered out.

"And you didn't answer my question. Do you still have nightmares?"

"Not the same ones I used to have." Terrible dreams about being back in that little cabin, only she'd been alone there. Hayden had never appeared. She'd been tied up, helpless and then the man in the baseball cap had opened the door. "Now I dream about my cases, about the victims that I don't get to find in time." They haunted her. "Excuse me." She stepped around him.

"You did find a lot of them in time, though," he said. "You've saved lives, Jill."

Her shoulders stiffened.

"The little boy in South Carolina, the one who was taken after he got off his school bus…you got to him in time."

She'd found the boy in the trunk of his abductor's car. The kid had been terrified, shaking and ice-cold because a sudden winter storm had swept into the area. "Another few hours," she said, remembering, "and I think Matt would have frozen to death."

"And what about the little girl in Mississippi? The one that was taken from her family's campsite?"

"Lula Jane."

He nodded.

"We got her right before the woman who'd abducted Lula…" Jill's lips pressed together. "We found Lula Jane before that woman had a chance to use her knife on the little girl."

"Those are just two of the kids you've saved.

I read about your work in articles on the internet. I know there are dozens more."

Her gaze met his. "And dozens lost. You know what hits you worse? The ones that you find too late. They're the ones who wreck you, Hayden. They're the ones who haunt you." She paced toward her bedroom.

"So you *do* still have nightmares."

Her fingers pressed to the wall near her door. "Only some nights."

Silence. Then… "I still have them, too."

She glanced over her shoulder. "After all you've done, Mr. Navy SEAL, I don't—"

"The worst nightmares are about you. Not getting to you in time. Finding *you* dead on the beach."

Her breath chilled her lungs.

"But I have new nightmares, too. About my missions. About friends that fell in battle. About detonations going off right in front of me as I watch people I cared about get blown apart. Those dreams are always silent…weird, but… I think it's because when the explosions really happened, I couldn't hear anything for a few seconds after them. Usually about ten seconds. I counted once…it took ten full seconds before I could hear the screams."

She closed her eyes. How many times had she been awake late at night, wondering about him? Worrying? She'd gone to her contact at the CIA just so she could find out where he was. She'd bent rules because she'd needed to know he was safe.

Alive.

Her eyes slowly opened. "Those dreams sound like pure hell." She made herself face toward her bedroom again. But she didn't step inside. She didn't leave Hayden, not yet.

The floor groaned beneath his feet. She knew he was coming toward her, that he was just in front of that TV. She didn't move, and a moment later, she felt his fingers curl around her shoulder. Hayden turned her toward him. "Hell is not having found you. Being stuck in a nightmare where you're dead. Like I told you, Jill, those are the worst ones for me."

The way he talked, the way he looked at her... it was as if no time had passed between them. She was a nineteen-year-old kid. He was the twenty-one-year-old who'd grown up so fast. Right then, he still stared at her as if she were his entire world.

He'd certainly been hers.

The heat from his touch seeped into her. Her heart was drumming in a too-fast rhythm. Her breath was rushing from her lungs. She looked into his eyes, and Jill wanted.

Simple fact.

She wanted.

His touch. His kiss. His body, in hers. She wanted to get lost in the pleasure she'd known with him. Yes, she'd had other lovers since him. Ten years was a very long time. But…she'd always compared those men to Hayden.

Always, damn it, and she'd hated herself for doing that.

Hated herself for waking in the night and wishing that he were there beside her.

Jill wet her lips. His eyes seemed to heat as he followed the quick, nervous movement of her tongue. It was time for another true confession between them. "Sometimes, I feel like I'm just going through the motions. Doing my job, going to work, hanging with my friends…doing everything that I'm supposed to do because that's what a normal life is." She could hear the thunder of the waves outside. "But then I realize that I'm almost numb. Everything is happening, and I'm just…watching. Not feeling."

His fingers tightened on her shoulder.

"And then I came back to Hope and you were here. I looked at you, and feelings slammed into me." So many that she'd thought she would be crushed beneath them all. "I look at you, and I want you, Hayden."

His lips started to curl.

But Jill shook her head. "That's dangerous."

"I would never be dangerous to you."

He would be absolutely lethal to her. She'd survived one heartbreak from him. Was she up to another? *Don't give him the chance to touch your heart again. Keep it just business between the two of you. Focus on the case. Play it safe.* "I want you, but you terrify me."

Pain flashed on his face. "That's the last thing I want."

"You're one of the few people…" She swallowed and tried again. "You're one of the few people in this world that can hurt me." *Brutally. Completely.* "I promised myself I wouldn't be hurt again, not by you."

She needed to get away from him. Needed to go in her bedroom. Shut the door and collapse. She was weaving on her feet, far too exhausted for this conversation. Actually, her exhaustion was probably the reason *why* she was having this talk now. Because her barriers were broken. Gone. And she was baring her soul to him.

I shouldn't. I need to stop.

"I promise… I swear…" His head dipped toward her. "I will never hurt you again. You can count on me, Jill. Always." His lips pressed to hers.

Back away. Back away. That little order whispered through her head, but Jill found herself leaning toward him, opening her lips and kissing him back.

Because when you live in numbness...well, is that really living?

Her tongue slid out and traced over his lower lip. He gave a low growl in his throat, and that deep, sexy sound just urged her on. She found herself leaning up on her toes as her hands pressed to his chest. She could feel the hard expanse of muscles beneath her touch, could almost feel the drumming of his heartbeat.

The frantic rhythm matched her own.

The kiss deepened. The passion heated. The desire mounted. Her breasts were aching, her nipples tight. She wanted to rub her body against his. Wanted to just let go...

His hand slid down her side, curled fingers over her hip.

He nipped on her lower lip. A quick, hungry little bite that made her gasp.

His tongue thrust into her mouth. He tasted her. Seemed to savor her. The need she felt for him deepened. The desire burned hotter.

It would be so easy to give in...right then. Right there. To keep kissing him. To strip away their clothes. To move into the bedroom.

There wouldn't be any numbness then. There would only be pleasure.

But...

What happened when the pleasure ended? When the sun rose?

When one of them had to walk away again?

Would the pleasure be worth the pain?

She didn't know. She—

He stepped back. His breath sawed out of his lungs and his glittering stare swept over her face. "I want to be clear on a few things."

She wanted his mouth back on hers.

"I will never hurt you again."

Her lips pressed together. She could still taste him.

"I will never let you down."

He'd only let her down once before. Unfortunately, that letdown had been epic.

"I *will* be the man you need."

She needed to step away. Before she crossed a line that went too far, for them both. She turned toward her bedroom, slipped across the threshold and started to shut that door. But then, Jill stopped. Something was wrong. Something about the way he'd said that last line.

"I will be good enough for you," Hayden promised.

She looked up at him. "You always were."

But his smile…it was a little cold. A little cruel. "You were the first person to look at me… *and see me*, Jill. Until that day on the pier, I was treated like trash by everyone in this town. Hell, even your grandmother thought I was trouble. They *all* thought that."

Her stomach was knotting.

"My father…"

She tensed. Hayden never talked about his father. *Never.* That was his one rule. She'd heard the stories growing up, but she'd never pressed him because every time she heard a whisper, she'd seen pain flash in Hayden's eyes.

"He was a killer. Before the kidnapper came to Hope, my father *was* the worst thing to ever happen to this town. He abused my mother, gave her more black eyes than I could count, and one drunken night, he robbed two tourists on the beach. Shot one guy in the chest…"

"Hayden—"

"I was always *his kid*. The killer's kid. The drunk's kid. The boy following in his father's footsteps. Because you know what I did?"

"Stop." He was hurting. He didn't need to tell her more. Not anything more. She just wanted Hayden's pain to stop.

"I stole when my mom and I had no food. I took things…from other kids when I didn't have clothes. Stole their gym equipment. Stole their fancy school supplies." His lips twisted. "I took what I wanted, and Sheriff Peek? He'd paid more than his share of visits to my house."

"That's in the past, Hayden. It's *always* been in the past for me."

"You know why I was on that pier?"

"Hayden—"

"I'd just gotten word that my dad had been killed in prison. My mother had drunk herself in a stupor after that, blaming herself. Like it was *her* fault the jerk had used his fists on her. I was on my own. I had nothing, *no one*. I was standing on that damn pier, looking into the water below and wondering…why the hell am I even trying?"

"Hayden—" She *hurt* for him. She'd tried to steel her heart against him, but this was Hayden. Beneath the anger she'd harbored for so long, the connection was still there. She knew it always would be there. Some bonds went too deep to ever be erased.

He stalked toward her. His dark eyes seemed to burn. "Whispers followed me everywhere. I couldn't go into any store without clerks watching me, thinking I was about to steal from them. I was trouble. The punk kid. The guy who was going to turn out to be just like his father."

Her hand reached out and she grabbed on to his arm. Held tight. "You are nothing like him."

"Because of you."

Her lips parted.

"You came to me on that pier when I had

nothing. When I was at my worst. A pretty girl with dark red hair, and you smiled at me. You stared at *me*. Not the piece of trash that everyone thought I was. You saw me."

She had to swallow the lump in her throat. *I always saw you, Hayden.*

"Then in a flash, you were gone. You'd wanted to be my friend, and I drove you away. I went after you and I saw him taking you." A muscle flexed in his jaw. "I knew right then, I would do anything to get you back. No one was going to take you from me. No one was going to hurt you. Not while I was around."

And he'd come for her. Later, she'd learned that he'd stolen a bike from the pier. That he'd ridden after the SUV, desperate to get to her. The bike's chain had broken, and he'd run until he found her. He'd stayed on her trail, he'd broken into that little cabin and... "He could have killed you, you know that, right? If he'd found you coming into that cabin."

He just stared down at her.

"Hayden?"

"You were worth the risk."

Her lips were trembling so she pressed them together. She was still holding on to him. Far too tightly. She should let go.

"When we went back to town, people saw

me differently then. Not trash. You turned me into a hero."

Anger had her shaking her head. "I didn't do anything. You did it. They just finally realized who you really were." Hayden had always been her hero.

That was why it had hurt so much when he turned away.

I'm leaving, Jill.

Those words had locked her heart in ice.

His hand lifted and curled under her chin. "You never got it, did you?"

"Got what?"

"They were right about me. I knew it, deep inside. I saved you because I'm a selfish bastard. You were mine, and I wasn't letting anyone take you away. Even back then, as young as I was, I looked at you, and I knew."

She shook her head.

His thumb feathered lightly over her jaw. "You deserved so much better. I knew it. I left. I joined the navy because I wanted to be the man you deserved."

Her eyes widened. "Hayden...that is such bull."

He blinked. "What?"

"You think I didn't know who you were?" Now her hand moved and pressed her fingers right over his heart. "In here? You think I didn't know you heart deep? Soul deep? You were my lover, Hayden. And I always knew exactly who you were." She paused, then said the truth she'd carried for so long. "You were mine."

Then you broke my heart.

His jaw hardened. "I wanted to be the man you needed. Holding you back from your dreams… that wasn't the way to go. I needed to prove myself."

He'd never had anything to prove to her.

"I was going to be more than just his kid. I became more."

A war hero. A man who'd battled mission after mission. An elite SEAL.

"The problem was…" Now his hand slid away from her cheek. "I learned I was far too good at a particular job."

Her heartbeat seemed too loud in her ears. "What job was that?"

His dark gaze held hers. "Killing."

LIGHTS WERE ON in Jillian West's rental cabin. A blaze of lights that glowed in the night. He drove past the cabin, barely slowing. Now wasn't the time. He had to think, had to plan. Jillian could *not* come back and wreck things. It just couldn't happen.

She had to be stopped. If she went prying into

the past, she'd destroy far too much. Too many lives were on the line.

She has to be stopped.

His headlights blazed ahead as he accelerated. He'd think of something. He'd handle this. After all, it was his turn to do the job. His turn to protect the family.

Jillian wouldn't hurt anyone that he cared about. She wouldn't destroy the life he'd built.

He wouldn't let her.

Chapter Eight

I'm leaving.

Hayden stared up at the ceiling in Jill's cabin. The wind seemed to howl outside and the little cabin creaked a bit on its wooden stilts. The ocean waves roared outside and he just remembered...

I'm leaving.

They'd been on the beach when he told her his goodbye. She stared up at him, her green eyes stark, her face going slack with pain and shock.

He'd done that. He'd hurt her. The one person who mattered most in the world.

She'd buried her grandmother when she was eighteen. She'd spent months settling her grandmother's estate. She'd finally sold her grandmother's home, she'd gotten enough money to pay for her college. She had big plans for getting into the FBI. For starting her life, *their* life but...

I had nothing to offer her. He'd known the truth in his heart. She'd deserved so much better.

Two different paths. Two different lives. He'd seen it so clearly. She'd needed to follow her dreams, and he'd needed to prove that he could be more than his father's son. Needed to show that he was more than one act of courage on a desperate day.

He'd had to understand his own measure as a man. Had to see for himself. When he was pushed to the limit, what would he do?

But that day, standing on the beach, seeing Jill's pain…it had broken something inside of him. Something that hadn't mended right in all of the years since then.

Did she know…did she have any clue…that when he got leave back to the States, he'd always gone to her? Just to get a glimpse. Just to see her. Just to make sure she was all right.

Sounded stalkerish as all hell, he knew that. But he'd just needed to make sure she was happy. The world was better when Jillian was in it, he knew that fact for certain.

Once, he'd planned to approach her. He'd even gotten flowers. Lilacs, her favorites. He'd been going to her apartment in Atlanta but then he'd seen another man heading to her door. Another guy carrying lilacs. He'd thought Jill had moved on.

I won't stand in her way.

So he'd slipped into the shadows. Gone on to another mission. But she'd always been there in his mind and in his heart. No matter where he went, she was there.

He'd discovered she was far more than just some boy's crush. Not just a man's obsession. She was everything.

And he'd lost her...all on his own. No one had needed to take her. He'd—

Her bedroom door opened with a soft click. Hayden surged upright, his body instantly on alert. "What's wrong?" He leaped to his feet and hurried—unerringly—toward her in the dark. He'd always had good night vision. His hands reached out and curled around her arms. "What is it?"

"I still have bad dreams." Her voice was soft, husky. "Sometimes, I just... I have trouble sleeping."

He should let her go. She'd probably just come out for a glass of water or something and he'd practically jumped on her.

"You asked me before," she continued quietly. "And, yes, I still have those dreams."

So did he.

"But dreams didn't keep me up tonight."

Her skin was so smooth and soft beneath his touch.

"Fear kept me up."

Hayden shook his head. "Jill, you don't have to be afraid—"

But her soft laughter cut him off. "Everyone's afraid sometimes. Even FBI agents. Even big, bad navy SEALs."

He was still touching her. His fingers were lightly stroking her skin. *Get a grip, man. Let the woman go.*

"Do you know why I'm afraid tonight?"

Hayden cleared his throat. "I'm not going to let that guy get a second chance to—"

"I'm afraid that I've been numb for too long. Every case that I take—every victim I lose—the numbness grows more and more around me. I know I should feel more. I should be happy. Everyone should be happy, right? But I can't get that way. There's too much pain in the world. Too much darkness. I see it all around me, and I'm so tired of it." She moved her body closer to his. Her hand rose and curled around his neck. "I don't want to be numb any longer. For tonight, even if it's fleeting, I want to feel."

He was feeling plenty at that moment. Whenever she was close, the hunger he felt for her, the raw desire, was never far from the surface. But he needed her to be sure, because once they crossed this line...

There is no going back. Not for him.

Not for her.

Because he wouldn't give her up again.

"When I'm with you, the numbness fades away. I feel anger, I feel bitterness…"

That wasn't exactly sounding awesome.

"And I feel need. Desire." Her voice softened even more. "I want you, just as much now as I always did. That want burns past the numbness. You make me feel again." She rose onto her tiptoes and her body brushed against his. "Tonight, I want to be with you. Just tonight. A time to let everything else go and just…feel. Just be."

He'd give her tonight. He'd give her a thousand nights if that was what she wanted. His lips took hers, softly at first because part of him was afraid this was just a dream. He'd had plenty of dreams about Jill over the years. She'd come to him like this, soft skin, husky voice, sweet desire. He'd locked his arms around her in those dreams. His lips had pressed to hers…

And she'd vanished.

He'd woken on old cots, woken in darkened tents, safe houses on the edge of hell…woken without her.

She tasted sweet. Her lips were soft, her tongue tempting him.

She wasn't vanishing.

His hands slid down and locked around her hips. He brought Jill even closer to him, holding her tightly. The kiss deepened, hardened, and when she gave that faint moan in the back of her throat, the sexy sound that had always driven him wild, Hayden knew there was no turning back.

She wanted to feel? Wanted to lose the numbness around her? He'd make sure to give her more pleasure than she could stand. He'd give her every single thing that he had.

And it would just be the start for them.

Her breasts pressed against his chest. He'd ditched his shirt, and the soft cotton of her top was the only shield between them. Her nipples were tight, hard, and it had been far too long since he'd tasted them.

"Be sure," Hayden gritted out as he pulled his mouth from hers. But then he just started kissing a path along her throat. She'd always liked that. "No going back…" This wasn't a one-time thing for him. Jill would *never* be a one-night stand.

"Make love to me," Jill said.

Hayden was lost.

He picked her up, held her so easily and took her back to the bed. A faint light glowed from her bathroom, spilling onto the bed. He put her down there, right in the middle of the covers. She wore a little black T-shirt and a pair of tiny gray shorts. The long expanse of her legs was revealed to him. She'd always had truly killer legs. He stood by the edge of the bed, staring down at her, and then he had to touch. His fingers trailed up her leg. Starting at her knee, moving up higher, sliding over her silky thigh.

He heard the hitch of her breathing and then Jill was parting her thighs for him. Trusting him so completely.

His arousal shoved against the front of his pants. He wanted to ditch those pants and get naked on that bed. He wanted to be *in* her. But Hayden was going to make sure Jill had more pleasure than she could stand. That night, with him, she would feel every moment. His fingers slid between her legs, caressing her so carefully through the soft fabric of her shorts. She arched her hips toward him. No hesitation, just trust.

The way it had always been between them.

Hayden's gaze slid over her body. She was so perfect to him. Did she understand that? Every single inch of her had been burned into his brain. He remembered exactly what she liked, exactly how to touch her, where to touch her. How to drive her wild.

Jill wanted to feel? He'd make sure he gave her all that she needed.

His hand slid away from her.

"Hayden?"

"We're going slowly." Because he'd savor her. "It's been a long time, and I need to touch all of you." Every single inch. He reached down and caught the hem of her shirt. He pulled it over her head and tossed it into the corner of the room.

Her breasts were pebbled, hard peaks and thrust toward him. In the weak light, he couldn't see her nipples clearly, but he remembered the soft pink hue. Hayden slid onto the bed. He bent over her and he touched her nipple with his fingers, a careful caress. Then he put his mouth on her nipple. Licking her, tasting her.

Not so careful, not with the desire firing his blood and every instinct he possessed ordering him to *take*.

She gave a little gasp and her fingers flew to curl around his arms. He liked the faint bite of her nails. Loved the way she held so tight to him.

But they were only getting started.

Hayden took his time with Jill. Licking, kissing, caressing her. He worshipped her breasts. Couldn't get enough of her. She was whispering his name, her hips rocking against the long length of his arousal, but it wasn't enough for him. He needed her to go wild.

Then he'd follow her.

Hayden's hand slid down her body. He slipped down her shorts, moving so that she could kick them away. Her shorts and the thin scrap of underwear that she'd worn. Then he was touching her heated core. Soft, wet and ready. He nearly lost his damn mind.

"Hayden, I don't want to wait." Her voice was the purest temptation in the world. "It's already been too long."

Ten years too long. Ten years of memories and dreams. Ten years of being without her.

No more. He had her back in his arms next to him. He wasn't letting go.

He stroked her delicate sex. Pushed her to a fever pitch of desire. Her hands slid over him. Touching him and amping up the dark need that surged within him.

His mouth kissed a trail down her stomach. Down, down he went, driven to taste all of her. She smelled so good, felt so soft. Heaven in his arms. Heaven after too many years of hell.

He put his mouth on her, right on the center of her need, and Jill came apart for him. He felt her pleasure, heard it in her voice as her hips surged against him. There was no shyness, no restraint. Not between them. There was only pleasure.

And they were just getting started.

He kept stroking her, kept kissing her, as her climax crested. No one else was like Jill. No other woman had ever come close for him. She consumed him.

Was an addiction to him.

He eased back from her, still savoring her

taste, and Hayden stared down at her. He wanted to sink deep into Jill, wanted to bury himself in her and erase the years of darkness that lay between them. "Don't move," he ordered, aware that his voice was gravel rough. His control was too thin. He was about to go over the edge any moment.

Have to protect her.

Always.

Hayden rose from the bed. He ditched his pants and underwear, then grabbed the wallet from his back pocket. He'd had an optimistic moment earlier and he had a condom with him. He put on the condom in pretty much record time and was back with her in an instant.

He positioned his length at the entrance to her body. His hands caught her hips and—

His gaze met hers. Her breath came in quick pants. Her body was open, waiting, his.

I need her to be mine again.

Because he'd never stopped belonging completely to Jill.

Hayden thrust into her, sinking deep, and his control shattered. Her legs wrapped around his hips, her nails scraped over his arms, and they drove toward completion. Faster, harder, she met him, thrust for thrust, her soft words urging him on. She licked his throat, kissing him just over the wild beat of his pulse point. She remembered what he liked. She—

Jill bit his earlobe. A quick, sexy nip. She whispered to him, dark and sexy promises, things they'd done, things they would do.

Her body was so tight and hot and he knew she could feel his release mounting, he couldn't hold back.

Jill, I need you to let go first. I need you to go wild. To feel—

Her body stiffened beneath him. "Hayden!" A quick, sharp cry and her delicate inner muscles squeezed him as her climax hit.

He followed her, pumping into her body and holding her tighter than he'd ever held anyone or anything. The pleasure ripped through him, making his heart pound too fast and hard, consuming him and reaching soul deep.

He bent forward and kissed Jill, tasting her pleasure, savoring the pure heaven of her and feeling—for the first time in ten years—peace.

Because he was right where he wanted to be. Right where he needed to be.

With Jill.

And he'd be damned if he'd ever let her go again.

SUNLIGHT TRICKLED ONTO the bed. Jill's eyes opened slowly, and then she blinked against that brightness. When the sun rose, it always came pouring right through that window and onto her bed.

Only I'm not in the bed alone. Not today.

Her head turned.

Hayden.

His eyes were still closed, his dark lashes looking incredibly long. His blond hair was tousled, courtesy of her fingers. They'd fallen asleep together, in each other's arms, as if it were completely natural.

His arm was still over her stomach, she was still cradled close to him. As if…as if he hadn't wanted to let her go, even in sleep.

Her breath slowly eased out as she stared at him. So handsome with such strong features. That hard jaw…she'd always loved to kiss it. Time had been kind to him. He was more rugged, harder and so incredibly sexy with that faint stubble.

Her gaze slid over his body. The broad shoulders and tan skin. The covers were pushed near his waist; the guy had always seemed to run a bit hot, she remembered that, and…

Scars.

Jill stiffened.

She knew Hayden's body—well. Knew just how to touch him. Knew just what he liked.

Some things, a lover didn't forget. *Especially when the lover is your first.*

But the scars on Hayden, they were new.

Not just one scar. Not two.

She'd touched him last night. She'd felt the raised skin beneath her fingertips, but she'd been so far gone she hadn't stopped, hadn't realized—

"They look worse than they are." His voice was a deep, sleepy rumble.

"Bull." Now her hand reached out and traced those scars again. First the long, twisting scar that was near his heart. "Was this from a knife?"

"Machete."

Her heart stuttered.

"It didn't go in deep enough to do serious damage."

The damage looked pretty serious to her. "How many stitches did you get?"

"I was in the field, stitched it up myself...don't really remember how many...was just trying to stop all that blood."

Her eyes closed as she imagined that scene. "I... I didn't know." That little tidbit hadn't been in the files she received. Jill made her eyes open. Her hand drifted to another scar. Rounded, puckered. "Gunshot." She knew that one.

"Yeah."

"This one, too." Her hand rose to his shoulder. His gaze held hers. "Barely a flesh wound."

"You are such a liar." She started to pull her fingers back, but his hand rose, catching hers and holding tight.

"They don't matter. I healed. They're in the past."

But seeing them *hurt* her because...*because he could have died, and I would have been an ocean away.* "You could have told me about them. Told me that you were hurt."

His jaw tightened. "I didn't want you to waste your worries on me."

Waste her—

Jill yanked her hand away from him and rolled from the bed. She didn't bother grabbing a sheet to cover herself. She just needed to get away from him before she *exploded* and—

"What in the *hell* happened to you?" His voice was lethally soft.

She stilled.

Then she realized...*my back.* It was such an old injury that she'd almost forgotten. Her first big case as an FBI agent and her first hit.

Her shoulders rolled back. "Don't 'waste your worries on me,' okay? It was nothing that a few stitches couldn't fix." She strode toward the bathroom.

She didn't make it. Hayden had leaped from that bed and closed the distance between them. His hand curled around her shoulder and he whirled her to face him. "You were shot." His eyes glittered down at her.

"Yes, well, it happens in the line of duty some-times, but, apparently, you were hit more than I—"

"When."

Oh, now he was going to get all worried? He acted as if it were nothing for him to get injured, but she got one gunshot wound, and suddenly the world was ending. "My first case as an FBI agent. Back then, I made the mistake of think-ing that a father couldn't hurt his own child, that there was no way the man sobbing so hysteri-cally could be a killer... I was wrong." She'd turned her back on him at the wrong time. "It's a mistake I haven't repeated."

"You should have *called* me."

Did he even hear himself? Did Hayden see the craziness? She shouldn't be worried about him, but he was practically enraged over her injury. "I had my fellow agents at my side." Her lips twisted as she remembered. "And my partner back then, Steve Quick, he even brought lilacs to me when I got home."

Hayden let her go. Stumbled back as if he'd suddenly been burned.

"As much fun as this naked conversation is," Jill murmured. "Excuse me." Then she went into the bathroom and closed the door behind her with a very distinct snap. She waited a moment, flipped the lock and her shoulders sagged.

He'd been hurt. She'd been hurt. Both so far apart.

When I was in that hospital, I wanted him with me.

When he'd been on the battlefield, had he—

"Jill?" He rapped against the door. "I'm... sorry."

For what? She didn't move.

"I never wanted you to worry about me. Never wanted to burden you."

Her back teeth clenched. *I never thought of you as any burden.* She grabbed her robe and yanked it on. She tied the belt with a nearly vicious twist of her hands.

"When I was shot... I lay in that medic unit, and I thought of you."

Her hands stilled, clenching the belt.

"When that guy came at me with the machete, when it sank into my chest, my one thought was... I don't want some guy in a government suit showing up at Jill's door, telling her about my death. I don't want Jill crying over me. I don't want her hurt."

She opened the door.

He stood there, wearing his pants, his face tight, and his eyes even darker than normal. "You were the one I listed as my emergency contact. Just you. I mean, my mom is dead. There is no other family. *You* were my family."

And he'd been hers.

"While I was overseas…" He gave a rough laugh. "I wrote about a hundred notes that I never mailed to you."

"Why not?"

"Because I thought you were moving on. That you'd gotten a great life, the life you always deserved and that you were free of the past."

Free of him?

"June 14."

She had no idea what that date meant. It wasn't some anniversary for them—

"That was the day I came to your apartment, wanting to ask you for another chance. Only there was this guy with dark hair, wearing a fancy suit, and he was at your door, with lilacs in his hand."

Jill sucked in a deep breath. *June 14.* She'd been shot in early June, she couldn't even remember the exact day but—

"Were you hurt then, baby?" His voice was so rough. Ragged. "Were you in there hurting, and I just walked away?"

She couldn't speak. Actually couldn't find the words to tell him that, yes, she'd been released from the hospital then and Steve had come to check on her.

Pain flashed on Hayden's face as he seemed to read the truth from her expression.

"Hayden…"

He swallowed and backed away. "I… I should go check in at the office. See if any of the deputies—"

"We should start over." The words just came out.

He stilled.

"Not look at the past. At what we did to each other. At what we didn't do." *I wish I'd been there when he needed me.* "Why don't we just see what happens?" One thing was certain—crystal clear after last night—she didn't just want to walk away. Not again.

"You…want me?"

Now she had to laugh. "Wanting you is always easy."

The way his expression changed…the way his eyes fixed on her mouth.

"I love your smile," he rasped.

Her smile faltered.

"Don't." His hand rose. His finger traced her lips. "It makes me feel good. I missed your smile."

Her breath whispered against his finger.

"I want to start over," he said, giving a hard nod. "Hell, yes."

A weight seemed to lift from her heart. She

didn't want to wallow in their past or in the pain there. She was feeling again—and she liked that, but she didn't want to feel sorrow, not for either of them. Time to try something new. Time for something better.

His hand moved from her lips to her cheek. He was so warm and solid and strong before her. No ghost, no memory, no dream.

Hayden.

He bent his head and kissed her.

VANESSA GRAY HUNCHED her shoulders and pushed her hands into the pockets of her sweat-shirt—or rather, into the pockets of her brother's borrowed sweatshirt. It was huge on her, dwarf-ing her small frame, but she loved to wear it any-way. NAVY was emblazoned on the front of the shirt, and it was so soft. Whenever she wore it, she always thought of her brother, Porter, and she felt better.

She really wanted to feel better that day.

The sun was slowly rising across the sky. Whenever possible, she liked to come down to the beach and watch the sunrise. It made her feel peaceful.

She could use some peace.

Her parents were fighting. Again. She knew all of the signs. Her mom was about to leave her stepdad. *Another one bites the dust.* Her mom fell in love fast. But the problem was that she also fell out of love fast. Four marriages in eight years was proof of that.

And Vanessa knew she'd soon find herself in another town. Maybe this time, there would be no ocean view. No view of the rising sun.

So she figured she'd better enjoy it while she could.

The sand rubbed against her bare legs. She was wearing shorts and a sweatshirt, and she didn't even care if she looked silly. Her legs spread in front of her and the cold water came to lap against her toes. Vanessa started to smile—

"You're out early."

Her breath sucked in on a sharp inhale. She turned her head, jerking it to the right, and she saw a man standing there. Tall, wearing a black coat. A baseball cap was perched on his head and his sunglasses tossed her reflection right back at her.

"I like to see the sun come up."

"So do I." He flashed her a reassuring smile. "Peaceful, isn't it?"

Her shoulders relaxed. He seemed friendly enough, and he didn't seem to be giving off any creepy vibes. She just hadn't heard him approach because of the surf, so he'd caught her off guard. "Yes, it's peaceful." She started to trace circles in the sand with her index finger.

"Do your parents know you're here?"

Her finger stilled. She glanced at him from the corner of her eye. Was he about to get her into trouble? "They know." They had no clue. They thought she was still sleeping. They *were* still sleeping, courtesy of their late-night fight. She'd slipped out, the way she often did, and they hadn't heard a sound. Sometimes, she just needed time alone. Time to think.

Time to…

Escape.

He smiled at her. "Enjoy your morning." He gave her a little salute and then he headed off down the beach.

She watched him for a few moments. No one else was out. What a waste of a perfectly good morning. Sure, it was early, but some views were worth crawling out of bed a few hours early.

She waited until the sun had turned the sky a pretty pink, and then Vanessa stood up. She brushed the sand off her legs and then reached for her flip-flops. She carried them with her as she headed toward the parking lot.

Wonder what's waiting at home? Would there be angry voices today? Or…maybe silence. Dead, cold silence. She never knew exactly what to expect.

I wish that Porter was home. If he were home, then she wouldn't have to leave with her mom.

She could just stay with him. But she had no idea where he was. It had been so long since she'd gotten a letter from him.

She paused at the parking lot and slipped on her flip-flops. Her bike was locked to the rack. She just—

"I didn't know you were a liar, Vanessa."

Vanessa whirled around, a startled cry breaking from her mouth.

And he was there. The man in the ball cap. Smiling...a smile that chilled.

"Look, mister," Vanessa said as she backed away from him. "I don't know you and you don't know me, so—"

He took a step toward her. "I do know you. I've watched you for a long time. Just like I watch all of my girls."

OhmyGodohmyGod.

"I know your parents don't know where you are. I know you slipped away."

She turned and *ran* for her bike. But he moved fast, grabbing her by the hair and yanking her back. Vanessa opened her mouth to scream.

His hand slapped across her lips.

Chapter Nine

"So where do we go from here?" Hayden asked Jill as he stared down at her. He knew exactly where he wanted to go, back to bed, with her.

He was trying to take things carefully, trying not to screw up the tentative bond they were making. Jill was too important for a screwup.

"Where do you want to go?" she asked. Her lips were red from his kiss. She had such perfect lips. The sexiest mouth that he'd ever seen.

His fingers trailed over her arm. He *hated* that Jill had been hurt and that he hadn't been there. If he'd just walked to her door. If he'd shoved that other guy out of his way. "Life is all about the missed moments, isn't it?"

A faint furrow appeared between her brows.

"The things we don't do. The risks we don't take." The moments they didn't claim. "You ever think about that, Jill? How different life would be if one small thing changed?"

She swallowed. "Of course, I do. When I'm working a case…when I have to tell parents that their children won't be coming home…those moments are all I can think about."

The job was hurting her. He could see it.

"You're one of those moments for me," she continued. Her lashes lowered. "If you hadn't come after me, if you hadn't gone into that parking lot at just the right time, I know I wouldn't be here."

"You *are* here." He tipped up her chin to make her look at him. "You are exactly where I need you to be."

With me. Always…with me.

"Hayden—"

Her phone started ringing.

Jill gave a little laugh. "Someone has really terrible timing."

He didn't look away from her. "Let it ring."

Her smile was bittersweet. "I can't. It could be one of my bosses at the FBI. I'm supposed to be on vacation, but if it's an emergency…"

If it's a child who was taken. He nodded and stepped back. "Right. Get the phone."

She brushed by him and grabbed her phone, catching it right in the middle of the ring. He saw her frown as she glanced at the screen. Then she put the phone to her ear. "Agent West," she answered. After a moment, her frown deepened. "Hello? Is someone there?"

Jill waited a beat. Hayden stared at her.

She shrugged and hung up the phone. "Guess it was a wrong number." But she bit her lower lip and stared at her phone. "Unknown number," she murmured. She rubbed her brow with her left hand.

"Jill?"

She shook her head. "Sometimes, I can't turn it off, you know? I get suspicious of everything. Of everyone."

"You don't need to be suspicious of me." He wanted her to understand this. "You can trust me."

He saw surprise flash on her beautiful face. "Trusting you was never an issue. Despite everything, you are the one person I trust completely."

When she said things like that, the woman came close to bringing him straight to his knees.

Her phone rang again.

He saw the flash of Unknown Caller on her screen and his instincts made him say, "Turn on Speaker when you answer it." She'd been attacked in that very house. Now two calls, from someone who was hiding his identity—*not good.*

Her fingers swiped over the screen and she turned on the speaker. "Hello?"

Silence. No, not just silence. Wind?

"Who is this?" Jill demanded. When no one spoke, her delicate jaw locked. "You're speaking to an FBI agent so don't play some joke with—"

"I know who you are." A man's voice. Low. Raspy. "The problem is…you never knew who I was."

Jillian sucked in a sharp breath.

"No one was there to follow her…" Again, the voice was raspy, as if the guy was trying to deliberately disguise himself. "Pity. If no one saw her vanish…guess no hero will come to save the day for her."

Jillian's gaze flew up to connect with Hayden's. He saw the flash of fear in her eyes. For just a moment, she was the girl she'd been so long ago. That girl…she'd had the same look.

He'd hated it then.

It enraged him now.

But, in a blink, the fear was gone from her eyes. Her chin notched up. "Listen, buddy, I don't know who you think you are, but I am not playing games with you. I'll get a trace on your call, I'll triangulate your signal, and you will *wish* you'd picked someone else to harass—"

"You know this is no game."

Jill's breath rushed out. "You're saying you've abducted some girl? You've taken someone? Prove it. Prove—"

"She can't talk right now. You remember,

right, Jillian? You don't get to talk in the car ride. But maybe once she wakes up..."

His words trailed away and the call ended.

Sonofa— Hayden yanked out his phone. He called the station even as he heard Jill frantically making a call on her own phone. "This is Sheriff Black," he snapped when his call connected. "Have there been any reports of a missing girl in the area?"

"A missing girl?" Finn's voice rose sharply. "No, sir! I just came on duty but...no, nothing like that."

If she'd just been taken, there might not have been a chance for her parents to report her missing. He didn't think this was some prank call. Not with the attacks on Jill already. *No coincidence.* She was back in town and it sure looked like her abductor was, too.

And he'd taken someone else.

"I need to find that caller!" Jill's voice jerked his attention her way. She was pacing beside him, her phone at her ear. "Yes, jeez, yes, I did a reverse phone lookup immediately. The guy didn't answer—I don't know if his phone is shut off or what happened. That's why I need your help. Monitor his number. Triangulate the signal, track down the phone, do something! *Listen to me*...he just said a girl has been abducted!" She stopped and threw a frantic glance his way.

"Do I have a confirmation on a missing person in the city?"

He shook his head. No, they didn't have confirmation, not yet.

"I think he called me right after he took her. No, I do *not* believe this is some joke! Can you tell me where the call came from or not? Can you find him?" She seemed to hold her breath and then...

She shook her head.

"Sheriff?" Finn said, jarring him, and Hayden realized he'd just been holding the phone while he watched Jill. "What's happening? What can I do?"

"Put all of the deputies on alert. We have a potential abduction in Hope. A girl." Because the caller had said *she*. "I want patrols going out. I want cars on the streets and our deputies looking for anything suspicious." He planned on getting out right away to start a search. *No one was there to follow her.* Oh, hell, yes, he would be there. He'd tear that town apart if he had to do it. Conduct a door-to-door search.

If that guy wasn't just scamming Jill, I will find that girl.

He hung up the phone and saw that Jill had done the same. "No trace," she said, "but I've got the FBI monitoring my phone." Her steps rushed toward him. "Hayden, he's doing it again."

"We don't know that, not yet." But deep inside, he thought she was right. The guy was striking again. After all of those years...

You won't get away again.

"He killed Christy Anderson within twenty-four hours of taking her." Jillian was dressing quickly, frantically, while she spoke. "That means we're working against the clock."

He yanked on his own shirt, then hurried into the den to grab his socks and boots. He pulled on his shoulder holster and checked his weapon.

Jillian rushed out behind him.

He turned toward her, hating the fear that he saw on her face. "We don't have a missing person yet, Jill. No reports have come in to the station. We don't have a victim, not yet."

"We will," she said with certainty, her expression stark, and her eyes so deep and sad. "We will."

IT WAS THE bike that caught Jill's attention. She'd gone with Hayden as he began a search of the city and the beaches. There were still no reports of any missing children but...

But the bike caught her attention.

Same place. She and Hayden had just pulled up at the parking lot near the big pier. A few fishermen were out now, an older couple walking hand in hand. And...

And there was a light blue cruiser locked to the bike rack.

The bike could have belonged to anyone at all. Or…

She climbed from the patrol car and slammed her door. Her eyes wouldn't leave that bike.

"I see it," Hayden murmured as he came from the driver's side. "Come on." He marched toward the bike.

The handlebars were white and a light brown basket sat on the front of the bike. The lock was in place, securing the cruiser.

She turned, shielding her eyes from the sun. When she looked at the pier, she just saw the fishermen. The older couple. No kids. No girl.

When they'd left her cabin, they'd immediately come to this spot. Their first search point. She hadn't needed to tell Hayden to drive there, he'd gone instantly. *Because it all seems to be coming full circle.*

She'd come to Hope to get closure. She hadn't come so that another girl would become a victim. She'd never wanted—

Her gaze fell on the flip-flop. Just a dropped flip-flop on the concrete. It was about ten feet away from the bike.

"I'm going to talk to the men on the dock and see if they saw anything," Hayden said. Then he was gone, heading determinedly toward the men. She heard a few of them call out greetings to him.

The wind blew against her. It wasn't a cold day, not by a long shot, but a chill had settled bone deep for her. This was wrong. This *never* should have happened.

Her phone was ringing again.

She jerked when it vibrated in her pocket. Her fingers fumbled as she pulled it out and glanced at the screen. Unknown Caller. She waited a moment, one beat, two, just as she'd been instructed to do by her contact at the FBI. Then… "Hello?"

"She's awake now. Thought you might want that confirmation."

A girl screamed, a loud, desperate sound.

"Don't," Jill whispered. "Do *not* hurt her."

"I won't…"

She could see Hayden talking intently with one of the fishermen.

"In fact, Jillian, I won't do anything to her at all."

She took a step toward Hayden.

"Provided that you do *exactly* what I say."

She needed to keep him talking. She wasn't some terrified thirteen-year-old any longer. This wasn't her first, second or even third time to deal with a monster.

"Trade yourself for her, Jill. You give yourself to me, you take her place...and she can just walk away."

She was rushing toward Hayden. He looked up when her feet touched the pier and she saw the alarm in his dark eyes.

"Think about it," the caller said, and then he hung up.

She didn't have to think about anything. "We've got him," Jill nearly shouted to Hayden. *"We've got him!"* The FBI had been monitoring her phone. They should be able to find the jerk—they should have him.

It was the same cabin.

Jill let out a slow breath as she stared at the faded wood and the familiar, sloping roof. When she'd been a teen, she'd often snuck back to that place. The little cabin, nestled on the edge of the marsh. She hadn't actually gone inside during those days, though, because she'd been too afraid.

Since she'd come back to Hope, she'd thought about the cabin. She'd even intended to pay the scene of her crime a personal visit, but she just hadn't realized that she'd be returning *that* day.

"You're sure this is the spot?" Hayden asked softly. He was beside her, crouched down behind his patrol car. They'd gone in quietly, then parked behind the trees that surrounded the cabin.

"After he called me the first time, I got one of my buddies at the FBI to monitor my phone." Her heart was racing in a double-time rhythm, but her words came out calm, steady. "The call originated from *that* cabin."

A deliberate choice, she knew. The guy was sending her a message…

You're back. So am I.

And just where the hell had he been for all these years? Why start hunting again now? What had changed for him?

She had her weapon in her hand. Hayden had radioed in for backup during their drive over, but every moment that passed… *It's another moment that he could be hurting her.* "Are you ready?" Jill asked him.

Hayden's gun was at the ready. "Hell, yes."

"Then let's do this." Her breath whispered out. "I'll go in the front door, you take the back. The last thing we want is for him to slip away."

"Not again," Hayden gritted, his jaw locked tight. "He won't vanish again." He gave a grim nod. "Be careful."

Then he was gone, slipping away like a ghost as he kept to the line of trees. She wasn't surprised that he could move so stealthily. After all, that would have been part of his training. She knew he'd get to that back door and be ready. A perfect partner.

She kept covered as she made her way to the front door. She didn't want to present a target of herself. The guy in there—his phone calls had proved that he wanted vengeance against her. She wasn't about to give the perp a free shot.

If he wanted her, then he'd have to work for that hit.

She crept up the porch steps, moving slowly so that the old wood wouldn't creak beneath her feet. On the way over, Hayden had gotten Finn to pull up the property records on the cabin. It was currently listed for sale, a truth she'd noted when she glimpsed the slightly crooked for-sale sign near the front of the property.

The fact that the place was empty had probably made it even more appealing for the perp. *Was it like coming home for you, you sick jerk?*

The front door was ajar. A heavy lockbox— the type that Realtors always put on vacant homes—had been broken and lay smashed a few feet away. She eased out a slow breath. Jill couldn't hear any sounds from inside that cabin.

Not a single whisper.

She pushed open that door and slipped inside. No lights were on but sunlight streamed in through the windows. The front room was empty. The kitchen was covered with dust.

The hallway yawned before her, leading back

to the bedroom, the room she'd been held inside. It was a small cabin, tight, outdated.

A prison.

She crept down that hallway. The bedroom door was closed. Her grip on the gun never faltered as she approached the room. She had a sudden flash of waking in that small back room, of being on the floor. Of being tied, hand and foot.

She pushed open that door.

And Jill saw the phone that had been dropped onto the floor, dropped right in the spot she'd woken in years before.

"STEP INTO MY PARLOR," he whispered as she watched Jill vanish into the little cabin. She thought she was being so very clever. He'd figured she'd track his call. After all, she was the high-profile FBI agent now. Tracking him should have been easy for her.

He'd counted on that.

So he'd left a few…surprises for Jill. As soon as she went into the old house, he started to count. He figured it would take her a few moments to get inside. To get inside, then to find the phone.

He'd call her soon. And that call from him would be the last thing she'd ever hear.

WHEN HE'D BEEN a kid, Hayden had tried to pick the lock at the back of the cabin. A flimsy

lock, but he hadn't been able to get it open. He'd
scouted around the cabin, found that broken window and slipped inside of it in order to get Jill.

A new lock had been put on the back door.
Bigger, shiny. This time, he didn't try to pick the
lock open. He just kicked in that door.

If you're inside, you won't get out.

He ran in with his gun up, sweeping around
the rooms, looking for the man who'd thought
to raise fresh hell in *his* town.

But the hallway was empty. The little cabin
was too quiet. And when he went into the back
bedroom, the bedroom that had haunted his
dreams…

He saw Jill standing in the middle of the room.
She was staring down at a cell phone. When he
slipped into the room, she whirled, her gun aiming right at his heart.

"Easy." He inclined his head toward her. "No
sign of him out back."

"The girl isn't here. *He* isn't here." Her gaze
darted to the phone. "But he wanted us here. He
left that…"

And even as her words faded away, the phone
began to ring.

Jill reached for the cell phone.

But Hayden remembered another time, another place. A city where the sun blazed and
sweat always seemed to slicken his skin. A cell

phone had been left in a car near their safe house. It had started to ring. One of his team members had turned at the sound—

And hell had exploded around him.

Jill's hand had almost touched that phone. *"Jill!"* Hayden roared.

Her head whipped toward him. Her eyes had gone wide. He didn't say anything else—there was no time. He grabbed her hand and yanked her toward him. He was acting on pure, blind instinct, but the setup was too easy. An empty cabin, a phone waiting. Ringing.

"Hayden! What's happening?" Jill yelled, but she didn't fight his grip. She ran with him down the hallway.

He looked at her, his lips parted, and that was when he heard the explosion. A loud, reverberating blast that seemed to shake the entire cabin. He saw her face go slack with shock. She said his name once more, but he couldn't hear her voice. He couldn't hear anything but that terrible thunderous blast. Her lips were moving, though, and he knew clearly that in that last instant, Jill was calling out for him.

He grabbed her, locked his arms tightly around her, and they rushed toward the back door, even as a ball of flame seemed to roll through that house and come after them.

Smoke and flames raged as Hayden shoved

open that back door. Jill was coughing, choking, clutching tightly to him. They were almost clear. Almost free of the fire and the bomb that had been set.

The phone was the trigger, I knew it, I—

The windows exploded. The roof groaned and that little cabin was swallowed by the flames.

He leaped out with Jill, holding her tightly, and they slammed onto the ground.

IT WAS ALL about proper placement.

He smiled as he watched the flames destroy the little cabin. When he'd realized that the place was for sale, that no one lived in the cabin near the marsh, he'd known it was going to be the perfect location for him.

It had been easy enough to set his explosives. Put them in the right spot, and *bam.* The whole cabin would come down. Once the ceiling collapsed, escape from that cabin would be impossible. The flames and the smoke would take care of his prey.

"Guess you didn't get away this time," he whispered as he kept his eyes on the front of that cabin. Jill had gone in…

But she hadn't come out.

Finally, he'd eliminated the threat she posed. A threat that had hung over him for far too many years. No more looking over his shoulder. No more wondering about the FBI agent.

He turned away from the cabin. The smoke and flames would attract attention soon. Deputies would race to the scene. The firefighters would swarm as they tried to battle the blaze. And, oh, wouldn't it be too sad when the remains were recovered? The town hero, the sheriff, gone down trying to save his precious Jillian again.

Should have never saved her the first time. Hayden Black should have just minded his own business. If he had, he wouldn't be burning right then.

He tracked back through the marsh and got to his car. Just to be safe—because if Jillian had taught him one thing, it was the importance of securing your prey—he headed toward the trunk. He lifted it up and stared down at the girl inside. Bound, gagged, she wasn't a threat to anyone. Her hair trailed over the black carpeting in the trunk and she barely seemed to breathe.

He smiled as he stared at her. He'd known he could get Jillian to appear if he dangled new bait in front of her.

The girl had been the perfect bait.

He slammed the trunk. It was good to be back on his game again. Back on top.

No one can catch me. No one can stop me. I have the power now.

He wasn't some weakling. Not anymore. He was the boss.

And he'd just proved it. He'd taken out an FBI agent *and* a navy SEAL. He was unstoppable.

Unstoppable.

Chapter Ten

"Jillian!" Hayden knew they'd hit the ground too hard. He'd tried to roll and protect Jill with his body, but he wasn't sure he'd done a good enough job. Jill was slack in his arms, her head sagging back. There'd been so much smoke around them at the end. *"Jill?"*

His heart barely seemed to beat as he stared at her. Her eyes were closed and she seemed far too still.

Not good, not good. "Jill, don't do this to me." He held her tighter and rushed farther away from the flames. When he was sure they were clear, he put her down on the grass and smoothed the hair away from her face. "Jill?" His fingers slid down to her throat and felt the pulse there, it was racing, too fast. Too—

Her hands flew up and shoved against him. A fast, defensive attack that probably would have sent anyone else sprawling, but Hayden's reflexes had been honed by years of training, and he caught her hands, holding them in a tight grip, but making absolutely sure not to hurt her. *Never her.* "Jill?"

"I blacked out." She seemed stunned.

"Only for a few seconds." And that scared the hell out of him. "Did you hit your head?" He let go of her hand and began to lightly search through the thickness of her hair for a lump.

She swatted his hands away. "Not now."

Not now?

Jillian lurched to her feet. She took a step, then swayed. Hayden surged up and caught her. "Jill, damn it, what are you doing?"

But she shoved away from him. "He set that place to explode."

Uh, yeah, he had.

"You knew…" Her breath came in quick pants. "When the phone rang, you…you realized what was happening."

He'd suspected and he was real glad they'd hauled butt getting out of there. Another few moments…

Jill slapped at his shirt. "You're smoking."

Hell. He yanked off the shirt and tossed it to the ground. Hayden stomped on it, putting out the flames. He looked up—and saw that Jill was stumbling away.

She must have hit her head. She's weaving.

He grabbed for her again.

She pushed his hands away. *"He's here."*

Blood trickled down her temple. He swore. "Baby, you're bleeding." He needed to get her to a doctor.

But once more, she pushed against him. "Don't you see? He had to be watching, to make the phone call, to detonate the bomb. *He had to be close.*"

The cabin was burning so fast and hard around them, he could feel the heat of the flames lancing against his skin.

"He *has* to be here," Jill said. "He's watching." Her eyes seemed far too dark as she said, "He's always watching."

Hayden started to shake his head but…but he thought he'd just heard the sound of a car cranking. An engine growling to life. Jill's head whipped to the left at the same time, and he knew she'd heard the sound, too.

When she broke from him and ran toward the marsh they'd crawled through one dark and long-ago night, he didn't try to stop her. Instead, he raced with her, his feet pounding over the earth, his whole focus locked on that growling engine.

Jill's right. He would need to be close so he could watch the cabin. He lured her out here, he'd want an up-close view of the action.

The action… Jill's death.

Tires squealed. The guy was getting away. Hayden pushed himself to run faster and Jill was right with him. They shoved their way through the marsh and he caught sight of the back of the car, a big, sleek ride and—

"Tag number," Jill gasped. "Get…it."

The car vanished, whipping around the corner. Hayden yanked out his phone, ready to call for backup and get patrols out to find that bastard but—

When he yanked his phone out of his pocket, he saw that the device had partially melted.

Jill stood as still as a statue, her gaze locked on the spot that the car had been in moments before.

"Jill?"

She didn't move.

His hand curled around her shoulder. "Jill!"

Her body jerked. She looked up at him, blinking. "I… I think I know that car."

She knew the car?

Jill rubbed her forehead. "Everything's… hazy."

And the blood was still pouring from her temple. "Baby…" He pulled her close. He thought of how fast that fire had spread, how it had come at them, rushing and destroying.

They'd walked into the killer's trap. They'd barely walked out.

In the distance, he heard the scream of sirens. Help, backup, rushing toward the black cloud of smoke that filled the air. But that help would get there too late. The perp was gone, only...

His eyes narrowed. He'd gotten a partial on the tag, and Jill was right...the vehicle did seem familiar.

"He made a fatal mistake," Hayden whispered as he stared into Jill's eyes.

Two fatal mistakes actually.

One, the SOB had dared to hurt Jill.

And two, *you didn't take me out, jerk. You left me alive and that means I will be coming after you. Coming after you with everything that I've got.*

JILL'S HEAD HURT, her clothes were covered in ash and they were more than a little singed, and she knew a new assortment of bruises marked her body.

She'd almost died that morning. She *would* have died if Hayden hadn't pulled her out of that cabin. A rookie mistake, going for that phone. She should have known better.

I'm too close to this case. I'm acting on impulse. On emotion. I'm not doing the job the way I should.

Or, at least, she hadn't been. But she'd gotten

patched up by the paramedic on scene. She'd gotten her head clear. And—

I also got your tag number. When backup arrived at the cabin, Hayden had spouted off a description of the car they were after and he'd given the first three digits of the tag number. Even with her head feeling as if a sledgehammer had hit it, she'd been able to give the last four digits of that license plate.

She'd also been able to point the deputies in the direction of the owner because...

I know that car.

"Kurt Anderson," Jill whispered. "When he arrived at his father's place yesterday...he pulled up in a car just like that one." A big, black, sleek ride.

Firefighters were battling the blaze, but she knew they weren't going to be able to save the cabin. It was long past the point of saving.

And I'm glad.

She'd never understood why anyone would want to leave that cabin standing. If she'd had her way, it would have been torn to the ground years before. Instead, it had nearly destroyed her, again.

"We need to talk to Kurt," Jill said.

A muscle jerked in Hayden's jaw. Someone had tossed him a T-shirt to wear, one that had Harris County Sheriff's Office emblazoned on the front. "Finn is running the tag number. Let's see what—"

"*Sheriff!*"

Finn was running toward them.

"Sheriff, Agent West is right! That tag—it's for Kurt Anderson's 2015—"

Jill didn't hear the rest of his response. *Agent West is right.* That was all she needed to know. She rushed toward the nearest patrol car. When the paramedic had bandaged her bleeding temple, he'd muttered a bit about her needing stitches, but she was fine. Definitely good to go.

She yanked open the driver's side door of that patrol car. She looked inside. Where the hell were the keys?

"Don't even think about it." Hayden's hand curled around her arm and he pulled her back. "The only place you're going is into the hospital for those stitches."

He had to be insane. "I'm going after Kurt Anderson." *Kurt Anderson.* He'd done this? Part of her was shocked but…*you know families are always the first suspects. No one ever looked hard at Kurt for the crime. Maybe he killed Christy. Maybe Christy had never been taken by the same man who abducted Jill. Maybe Kurt had been his sister's murderer all along…*

"No, you're getting looked after. You probably have a damn concussion, the last thing you need is to be driving." His face was locked in tight, angry lines. "I hate to do this, but you're not giving me a choice."

What was he even talking about? Do what?

"Finn, take Agent West back to the ambulance. Stay with her while she goes to the hospital."

Her jaw dropped. He *wasn't* serious.

"I'm pulling jurisdiction on you, baby," he whispered. "Because I won't risk you."

She wasn't his to risk. She was an FBI agent. She was—

My vision's blurry, my knees are shaky and I can feel blood trickling down my temple again.

"I will bring him in," Hayden promised her as a muscle jerked along his clenched jaw. "But I have to know that you're okay."

"I'm fine," Jill gritted out the words. "Just… go. Don't let him get away. He…took someone. I heard her scream."

"We both heard her." He nodded. "I swear to you, I will find her. I won't give up."

Finn rushed toward them. "Ma'am?"

She hated this. "Forget me, Finn. Go with Hayden. He needs backup." And she'd be calling in some backup of her own, just in case. This wasn't going to be some jurisdictional war, that wasn't the way she operated. CARD team members didn't take over, they didn't huff and puff and steamroll their way over a local investigative team.

They worked together. They saved the victims. The victims were what mattered. "Go get her," Jill whispered.

Hayden squeezed her hand.

Then he was gone.

The paramedic hurried toward her. "Agent West?"

"Stitch me up," she ordered him. "Or find me someone else who can." She thought of Kurt, of Christy, of the way monsters could lie in wait for so very long. And she knew that they needed extra help. "And give me your phone." Because there was one special person at the FBI that she wanted by her side.

RAGE BURNED INSIDE of Hayden's blood. His hands had a death grip on the steering wheel and the thunder of his heartbeat echoed in his ears.

"Uh, Sheriff? Should you...maybe slow down a bit?" Finn asked nervously.

Slow down a bit? They were after a man who'd just tried to *kill* Jill. Another few moments, and Jill would have burned. They *both* would have burned.

He took the corner fast, making Finn slam against the side of the door. In his mind, he kept seeing Jill, lying so still, blood trickling down her temple.

Too close. Too close. Jill had almost been taken from him, and the fool who thought he'd gotten away with murder...

He was about to be in for a very unfortunate surprise.

Hayden slammed on brakes in front of the Anderson house. His sirens were blaring, his lights flashing. He jumped from the car and ran up the sidewalk. The front door opened and Theodore Anderson stood there, blinking owlishly at him. "Hayden Black? What the hell do you want?"

Hayden grabbed him, fisting his hand in the guy's shirtfront and he pushed Theodore back against the side of the house. "Where's your son?"

Finn had run toward the garage. "The car isn't here!"

"What car?" Theodore's gaze darted toward Finn. "Why's he looking in my garage? What's going on here?"

The rage bubbled even hotter inside of Hayden, as hot as the fire that had destroyed the old cabin. "Where. Is. Your. Son?"

"He usually goes for a run in the mornings. At the beach..." Theodore's face mottled. "Now get your hands off me!"

Kurt wasn't there.

"Your son's car was at the scene of an arson this morning." He let Theodore go but didn't back away. "Two people were nearly killed in that fire."

Theodore's eyes bulged. "What? No." He shook his head once. Hard. "No way, my son is *not* involved—"

"We think another girl is missing." No parents had come forward yet. They'd had the morning from hell, and no one had reported the girl as missing so far. "I need to find your son, *right now.*"

It seemed to take a moment for Theodore to connect the dots. Arson. Kurt's car. The missing girl...

Then the man's face seemed to crumple. "What? What are you saying?" But the terrible, dark suspicion was there, wide in his eyes. So clear to see.

"I'm saying I want to talk to your son. He's a suspect right now and I *want*—"

"There, Sheriff!" Finn yelled. "I see him!"

Hayden's head jerked to the left. Finn was pointing, and, sure enough, he saw Kurt. The guy was in the middle of the street, wearing a sweat-soaked T-shirt, jogging shorts and running shoes. Kurt's gaze was on the patrol car in front of the Andersons' house, but then his stare swung toward Hayden and Theodore.

He's going to run from me. Hayden knew it even before the guy turned on his heel and rushed back down the street.

The innocent don't flee. Hayden took off after the guy, rushing fast and hard, adrenaline fueling him. Kurt wasn't getting away. He'd told Jill he'd bring in the guy, and that was exactly what Hayden intended to do.

His feet pounded over the pavement. Kurt was fast, he'd had a head start, but Hayden was faster. In moments, he was right behind Kurt, and Hayden launched himself into the air. His body hurtled toward Kurt's, and he tackled the other man, sending them both flying onto the pavement. The cement tore into Hayden's forearms and ripped through his pants, but he barely felt the sting. All of his focus was on Kurt Anderson.

He pinned the guy beneath him on the ground. "Where the hell is she?" Hayden snarled.

Kurt tried to kick him, tried to headbutt him. What did the guy think? It was amateur hour? Hayden spun Kurt onto his back, cuffed him in seconds, and then yanked the heaving man to his feet. "Where is the girl?"

"What girl?" Kurt shouted. "Get the hell off me! Let me go!"

Hayden swung Kurt around to face him.

"Do you always run when you see a sheriff at your house?"

"I just— Let me go! I know my rights! You can't do this to me! I haven't done anything wrong!"

Finn pounded toward them. He had his gun out and pointed—a bit shakily—at Kurt.

"Don't hurt my son!" Theodore barreled after them.

Neighbors were peeking out, watching with wide eyes.

"Your rights?" Hayden laughed. "Fine, you have the right to remain silent, you have the right to an attorney, you—"

"Get these cuffs off me!"

Hayden stared into his eyes. "You should never have tried to hurt Jill." His voice was low, carrying just between them.

He saw it then—the flash of guilt. The nervous expression that told him he'd just hit pay dirt.

But then Kurt started sputtering. "I haven't done anything! I was just out for a run, I didn't—"

"Where's your car?" Hayden asked, cutting into his words.

Kurt blinked. "In the garage. I parked it there last night. I was out late, driving around. I came home and put it inside."

Hayden shook his head. "Try again."

"It's in the garage!" His frantic stare shifted to Theodore. "Dad, tell them—"

But Theodore wasn't saying anything.

"The car isn't in the garage," Hayden said as he locked his hand around Kurt's shoulder and pushed him toward the sidewalk. "But guess what? Jill and I saw you this morning. We saw your car right after you set that bomb. Couldn't get away fast enough, could you? Your mistake...you didn't take us out. *We saw you.*"

Kurt tried to wrench free and run.

Hayden just tightened his hand. "Where's the girl?"

"What girl?" Kurt was nearly yelling. "I didn't take anyone! I didn't do anything! Not to you or to your precious damn Jillian West! Let me go!"

"The only place you're going is to jail." Hayden stared at the man. "And all those secrets you've been keeping for so long? They're all about to be pulled out into the open."

Kurt blanched and he shot a guilty glance toward his father.

"You're done," Hayden said simply. "It's over."

Chapter Eleven

"I want to see him." Jill burst into the sheriff's station and flatly made her announcement. Finn jumped up when he saw her and rushed from behind the check-in counter. *"I want to see Kurt Anderson."*

"Are you okay, Agent West?" Finn's gaze darted to the bandage on her forehead. "I heard the paramedics took you to the hospital. Did the doctors release you?"

She had a concussion, she was in a furious rage and she was very, very much *not* okay.

Before she could say anything else, though, the door opened behind her. She looked back, and saw a woman with pale blond hair standing in the doorway. The woman wore no makeup, and her hair had been pulled back into a tight ponytail.

"I need to fill out a report," the woman said, her voice was shaking. Her hands trembled as she lifted them into the air and waved vaguely toward the check-in desk. "My daughter… I can't find my daughter."

Oh, no. Jill spun toward her even as she heard the echo of a girl's scream in her ears. "Ma'am? I'm FBI Agent Jillian West. I can help you."

The woman blinked her light blue eyes. "You're… FBI?"

Jill pulled out her badge. The wallet had stuck together a bit after the fire, but the badge was still good. "I specialize in missing persons cases. Children's abductions."

The lady backed up. "I think Vanessa just ran away. She wasn't abducted." Her smile was nervous. "I just need to see the sheriff, but…um, thank you, anyway." She started to walk around Jill.

Jill just moved, blocking her path. "How long has your daughter been missing?"

A crinkle appeared between the woman's brows. "I don't… I'm not really sure."

Jill didn't let her expression alter.

Red stained the woman's cheeks. "She was gone when I woke up this morning, but I figured she'd just slipped away for a bike ride. I mean… Vanessa does that. It's not like she's some little kid. She's a teenager—fourteen years old. I thought she'd be back but…"

But she wasn't.

The woman straightened her shoulders. "I had an argument with my husband last night. I know Vanessa heard it. She…she probably just got angry and is trying to punish me by disappearing for a while. I just need the sheriff to send out some patrols to find her and bring her back. Get her to stop this foolishness…" Her words trailed off as she stared at Jill. *"Why are you looking at me that way?"*

Jill released a slow breath. "What's your name?"

"Carol. Carol Wells, but my daughter is Vanessa Gray." She fumbled in her bag and pulled out a photo—it was one of those class photos with the overly springlike background. A girl with sandy-blond hair stared back at the camera, a small smile on her lips. "That's her. She's just—"

A door opened behind them. Jill heard the low creak and then the heavy thread of footsteps approaching.

"Sheriff Black!" Relief flashed on Carol's face. "I need your help! Vanessa's run away and I wanted to get a patrol to search the beaches for her."

Very slowly, Jill turned to face Hayden. The faint lines on his face seemed deeper, his expression dark. She knew that he'd taken Kurt into custody—Hayden had called her at the hospital and told her that much. But had he learned any-thing from Kurt yet? Anything like *where is the girl? What has he done with the girl?*

Carol rushed around Jill and grabbed Hayden's arm. "She's mad." She waved her hand in the air. "You know how teenagers get. I told her that I was thinking about moving. Maybe get-ting a fresh start somewhere else." Her voice dropped. "Ron and I aren't exactly getting along. We rushed into the marriage."

Jill stood there, her muscles tight, watching, waiting.

"Vanessa doesn't want to leave so she's acting out. But when you pick her up in your patrol car, that will scare some sense into her." She nodded decisively. "Yes, it will. So can you—"

Jill cleared her throat. "Carol doesn't know how long Vanessa has been missing." Then, because her suspicions were on high alert, Jill asked, "By any chance, does Vanessa own a blue cruiser? One with a brown basket?"

A wide smile spread across Carol's face. "She does! You—you've already found her?" Her gaze flew around the station. Finn watched the exchange, his face tense. "Where is she?" Carol blurted. "Is she in one of the offices?"

Where is she? That was the question they all wanted to know.

Hayden cleared his throat. "Mrs. Wells, I

think we need to talk." He took the photo from her hand, and then Hayden nodded toward Finn. "Get this out to all the patrols. I want every man and woman we've got looking for Vanessa."

Carol backed up a step. "What am I missing?" She whirled backed to Jill. "Why is an FBI agent even here now? What's happening?"

There was no easy way to say this. "We believe a girl was abducted this morning."

"*My* Vanessa?" Carol staggered.

"We don't know who was taken yet," Jill said quickly. "But we are going to find out." She wanted to get one-on-one with Kurt Anderson. She'd make him talk.

"And…" Hayden added, his voice a low rumble. "We *will* find your daughter, no matter what."

Jill's gaze jerked toward him. In the FBI, the agents were always taught never to make promises like that to family members. Never, ever make a promise that you couldn't keep.

Because sometimes, the victims weren't found. Sometimes, they never made it back.

HAYDEN PULLED JILL into his office and shut the door behind her. "You should still be at the hospital." She looked too pale, far too fragile to him. The scent of ash still clung to her—hell, to them both.

But Jill shook her head. "I'm stitched up and the doctors weren't keeping me there."

"Weren't?" Hayden repeated. "Does that mean they wanted to and you wouldn't let them?"

Her lips thinned.

"Jill…" She was killing him.

"I want to see Kurt Anderson."

"The guy isn't talking, Jill. He clammed up the minute I mentioned a missing girl. He's back in holding, and the man is not cooperating." Every time Hayden looked at Kurt, rage filled him.

"I need to see him." Her voice was calm, her stare unflinching. "You think I haven't dealt with my share of uncooperative witnesses and suspects? I know how to handle them. I can handle *him.*"

He knew she could. But…damn, it felt as if he were being ripped apart. He kept seeing the fire. Seeing *her…*

And I want to destroy the man who hurt her. But that wasn't what a sheriff was supposed to do. He was supposed to serve and protect. Deliver justice, not give in to his rage.

"Besides," she continued, tilting her head as she studied him, "Kurt wants to talk. The perp called me, remember?"

"Only so he could set you up to die." It had taken all of his self-control not to pound the hell out of Kurt. *You're the sheriff. You have the badge. It means something.*

It meant he couldn't give in to his fury. Not yet, anyway. Because somewhere out there, a victim needed them.

"How does this work?" Hayden asked her. "Your CARD team…what do you do? How do you—"

"There are certain investigative strategies that we always utilize. Normally, we immediately begin a search for any registered sexual predators in the area, we look for anomalies, we review video footage—" But she broke off, shaking her head. "This case is different. For this case, we begin with Kurt. He's our focus. You keep your men searching the streets for Vanessa, and you and I will make a run at him. We break him, and we find her."

He wanted it to be that simple.

"I've already contacted one of my most trusted friends at the FBI," Jill said. "She's on her way here now."

"Another CARD member?"

But her gaze turned shuttered. "No, not exactly. Samantha is…different. I think we need her talents here, not the other CARD members. Like I said, this case is different. We need different people to get the job done."

Okay. Well, he'd find out just how different

the woman was soon enough. For the moment, they had a perp to interrogate.

VANESSA OPENED HER EYES. Her head hurt. A terrible pounding that had nausea rolling in her stomach. She tried to sit up but…something was wrong.

She couldn't move her arms, not fully. Or her legs.

Terror clawed at her.

She opened her mouth to scream, and she realized that a thick cloth had been stuffed between her lips. The cloth was pulling at her cheeks. *It's tied around my head.* A gag.

Rough hemp bit into her wrists. She twisted and jerked. Someone had tied her up. Bound her hands and ankles, then looped that rope together so that she was trapped in a small ball, hunched over.

This can't be happening.

Tears leaked down her cheeks. She…she wanted her mom.

She wanted her brother.

She wanted *help.*

HAYDEN LED THE WAY back to the holding cell. Kurt Anderson was the only occupant back there, and when the guy saw him coming, he shot to his feet and headed toward the bars.

"Came to your senses?" Kurt demanded. "Good, now get me out—"

Hayden moved to the side so that Kurt could see Jill.

Kurt's words stopped completely and he just stared at her.

"Sorry," Jill murmured, not sounding the least bit apologetic. "Did I surprise you? After all, you worked so hard to kill me."

Kurt shook his head.

Hayden stayed silent. This was Jill's show. He wanted to see how far she could push the other man. *I'm betting damn far.*

"Hayden said that you haven't been cooperating with the investigation." She moved closer to the bars. "Why is that? After all, you've gotten away with your crimes for years. Surely you want to talk about them now. You want to tell everyone *your* side of the story."

His hands curled around the bars. "I haven't done anything."

Jill shook her head. "We saw you. Saw your car at the scene of the arson. Rather full circle, wasn't it? To lure us back to that particular cabin. To set the bomb to explode right then and there."

"I didn't rig some bomb! I wouldn't even know how to do that!" He jerked his head toward Hayden. "He's the ex-military guy. Isn't that his department?"

The shock—or at least, the shocked act—appeared to have worn off because Kurt was sure saying plenty now.

"And look, I don't know what's up with the car." Kurt was sweating. "It must have been stolen or something because no way was I driving it—I was out on my run, I swear!"

"The sad fact is…" Jill offered him a tight smile. "Anyone with internet access can get bomb-making instructions. And for someone like you—someone who has committed murder before, I'd think a little bomb making might be right up your alley."

"I didn't do it!" Spittle flew from Kurt's mouth. "Look, this is all a mistake." His gaze jerked toward Hayden. "I mean, come on, I was a kid back then, too. When Jillian was taken, I was your age!"

Jill stared at Kurt. "You aren't the man who took me."

His shoulders sagged. "Damn straight. Now get me out of—"

"He was older. Bigger than you were back then. But…" She gave a small shake of her head. "But that doesn't mean you aren't the man who killed Christy. You didn't take me, but you may very well have killed your sister."

Hayden's gaze sharpened on Kurt. Once more,

he saw the flash that could have been guilt appear in the guy's eyes.

"Everyone always assumed," Jill continued, her voice quiet, "that the man who took me also took Christy. But what if that wasn't the case?"

"I want a lawyer," Kurt snapped. "I want to see my father, too."

"What if…" Jill mused, watching him carefully. "There were two different attacks back then? My abduction…and Christy's death."

Hayden kept his expression locked. He didn't want to give anything away to Kurt, but what Jill was saying…

She thinks the guy may have killed his own sister. It took a special kind of sick mind to commit an act like that.

"Everything was fine for years in Hope, no abductions, no attacks, then I came back to town." Her lips curved down. "And one of my first stops was Christy's grave. Bet that made you angry, didn't it?"

Kurt was staring straight at her. "You should stay away from Christy," he whispered.

Jill nodded. "So I was told. But I didn't stay away. I showed up at your house. On your doorstep. I was talking to your father. You knew I was going to reopen the investigation, and you couldn't let that happen, could you?"

Kurt's hands fell away from the bars.

"So you had to stop me. You lured me to the cabin near the marsh and you set it to explode."

Kurt ran his hand over his face. "This isn't happening."

"You didn't want me finding out the truth about the past. You didn't want anyone to know the truth about Christy." Her voice had dropped, become sad.

Hayden realized she was manipulating Kurt, pushing at his emotions. She was good. Damn good. But Kurt hadn't broken, not yet.

Kurt's shoulders hunched. "I can't…"

"But Christy is gone," Jill continued, her voice still soft. Still sad. "There is nothing we can do for her now. The girl you took this morning… she isn't. There's still a chance to help her. To *save* her."

Kurt's hand fell. Once more, he looked over at Hayden. "You…you mentioned a girl."

Hayden gave a slow nod. *Yeah, I mentioned a girl, all right. Vanessa Gray. And her mother is currently sobbing in my office.*

"Where is the girl?" Jill asked Kurt. "I heard her scream when you called me on the phone. She was alive then." A pause. "Is she alive now?"

Kurt shook his head.

Hayden's heart seemed to stop. He couldn't stay silent any longer. "You killed her." The words were rough, guttural. He stepped forward, his hands fisted as—

"I didn't take anyone!" Kurt's eyes had flared wide. "I never took any girl today! I didn't set a bomb—*I didn't do this! It wasn't me!*"

Jill glanced at Hayden.

"I want a lawyer. Get me a lawyer!" Kurt pleaded. "I am not going down for this! I didn't take any girl today! I didn't do it!"

Jill turned away from him.

"Where are you going?" Kurt stuttered. "You're not leaving me here again?"

Hayden just stared at him. "You want a lawyer, then we'll get you one. But if that girl dies, if you've set her up to suffer while you're in here…" His teeth clenched. "I swear, you'll be sorry," he promised.

Then Hayden followed Jill out of the holding area, making sure to secure the doors shut behind them.

He took a few steps, then realized that Jill had stilled in that narrow hallway. He put his hand on her shoulder, and she turned to face him. "Something isn't right," she said.

There were a whole *lot* of somethings not right with that case.

"He's denying taking the girl today, denying the bomb…" She rubbed the back of her neck.

"But did you notice that he never denied being responsible for Christy's death?"

Hayden realized she was right. The guy had flinched, he'd flushed when she mentioned Christy and the idea of two separate perps, but Kurt hadn't denied guilt for his sister's death.

Damn.

"We're missing something," she said. "I know it. I need to talk to Samantha. She can figure this out, she can help us."

And he needed to find out the damn status on the hunt for Vanessa. The girl was *his* priority. His citizen, his responsibility. And every moment that ticked away…

"Let's set up a base of operations here," Jill decided. "We need to retrace Vanessa's steps, figure out where the killer could have taken her. Any other empty houses that are close by—cabins, beach rentals—we need to search them all."

Hell, yes, they did.

His hand tightened on her shoulder. "Everything we have on Kurt is circumstantial at this point." The truth grated. "If he sticks to his story about his car being stolen, if he can produce witnesses who saw him on his run, then the guy will be walking right after his lawyer arrives."

She swallowed. "I know…just…keep him as long as you can, okay? I'm telling you, he's holding back on us. I could see it."

So could Hayden.

She started to pull away, but he didn't let her. He brought her closer. They were alone right there, and he needed to—

I just need her.

His head lowered. His lips pressed to hers. Not a desperate, wild kiss. Soft. Careful.

Tender.

Emotion was in that kiss, all of the emotions he'd kept bottled up for far too long. When he thought of the danger around them, around *her,* he wanted to rage. "I can't let anyone take you from me." He bit off the words against her mouth.

Her hand pressed to his chest. "I am not going anywhere. I promise."

Promises were easy to make. But life was cold and hard and twisted, and fate could rip anyone's world apart.

She pressed another kiss to his lips. "Thank you, Hayden."

His brow furrowed. What was she thanking him for?

"You saved me today," Jill whispered. "I won't forget that."

He let her pull away. He *watched* her walk away, and Hayden shook his head. Jill just didn't get it. He wouldn't have left that cabin without her.

Not years ago.

Not that morning.

She'd saved him, long ago, and there was no way he'd ever let her suffer.

Chapter Twelve

Five hours later, Vanessa Gray was still missing. No one had seen her when she was on the beach. No one had seen her vanish from the parking lot.

No one had seen the girl at all.

Deputies were canvasing all of the vacant properties in the area. The news was running Vanessa's photo, and Jill feared they were running out of time.

Jill had established an on-site command post at the sheriff's office. She'd mapped out the locations of all registered sex offenders within a one-hundred-and-fifty-mile radius. Law enforcement personnel were en route to question all of those offenders. She was following standard CARD protocol but...

But this case is different. I don't think we're going to find some registered sex offender who has the girl. This case is deeper than that. Darker.

She looked at her phone. The guy had called

her before. He'd lured her to the cabin, and then he'd rushed away.

If...*if* Kurt Anderson was telling the truth, then the perp had set him up. He'd deliberately taken Kurt's vehicle. Why?

So that if he was seen, the authorities would focus on Kurt? Did the guy *want* them looking at Kurt?

Tension was heavy and tight in the back of her neck. This case was driving her crazy. She wanted to find Vanessa. Every time that she thought of that girl...

I see myself. Scared and alone in the cabin.

And it was just like the jerk on the phone had said. There was no one to rescue Vanessa. No one had seen her.

A knock sounded, a gentle rap against the side of her office door. The door was open, and Jill's head whipped up at the knock. She blinked, staring in surprise at the woman who stood in the doorway.

Samantha Dark gave her a slow smile. "You were expecting someone else?"

Jill jumped out of her chair. She was so glad to see the other woman that she almost hugged her, but protocol held her back. "I am so glad you're here."

Samantha Dark was *the* rising star when it came to profiling killers at the FBI. The woman's mind seemed to always be working, spinning, plotting, dissecting. Samantha took the darkest cases, the most gut-wrenching investigations, and the lady seemed to pull out the motives of the killers as if she were working magic.

Samantha's black hair was pulled back into a twist. Her golden eyes glinted as she shut the office door behind her. "You said you needed me, so that meant I got on the first plane available and got my butt down here."

Because Samantha was also a great friend. They'd first met at Quantico, and they'd bonded during training. Jill had known that she wanted to work the child abductions while Samantha had been bound for the behavior analysis unit. On day one, they'd clicked.

And, suddenly, Samantha was pulling Jill in for a tight hug. "I mean this in the nicest way," Samantha murmured into Jill's ear. "But you look like hell."

A shocked laugh escaped Jill's lips. "Thanks." She hugged Samantha, reassured to have the other woman there. Samantha had been there for Jill after she was shot on that very first case. She'd been there on the slightly drunk nights when Jill had broken down and spilled about Hayden.

She'd always been there, a true-blue friend.

Samantha eased back. Her gaze swept over

Jill's face. Samantha was beautiful, but Jill had noticed that she always tried to downplay her looks. No makeup. No too-tight or low-cut clothes. Just business, that was Sam.

Most days, anyway. Jill had seen her friend cut loose a time or two.

"I read up on your abduction on the way here," Samantha said, giving a slight nod. Her lips pursed. "But to be honest, I have to confess… I dug up your case file years ago."

She'd done what?

"You carry a lot of pain, Jill," Samantha murmured. "I've wanted to help you for a long time."

"A girl is missing." She backed toward the desk and handed Samantha the file she'd composed on Vanessa Gray. "He called me—the bastard who took her. I heard her scream."

Samantha began to rifle through the file.

"We have a man in custody. Kurt Anderson."

Samantha looked up. "Christy Anderson's brother?"

Jill nodded. "You *did* do your research." It was a bit unnerving to realize that—all along—Samantha had known all of the secrets that Jill carried about Hope. Samantha had known those secrets, but hadn't said a word.

"Like I said—" Samantha inclined her head "—I wanted to help you. Sometimes, Jill, your pain was like a cloak around you. And there's always a reason…"

"A reason?"

"Why we choose the paths that we take. You wanted to help children. That was your mission and burden. Your single focus. It only stood to reason there was a direct motivation for that desire."

Ah, there she went…*she's profiling me.* But two could play that game. "You only wanted to work with the serial killers, so what motivation do *you* have?"

Samantha's thick lashes lowered. "Maybe I understand them *too* much because I understand their darkness a bit too well." Then Samantha cleared her throat. "You think a serial is at work here, or you wouldn't have called me. You would have gotten some of your CARD teammates down here right away."

Jill bit her lower lip. "When I first talked to you, I did. Me, Christy Anderson…after the two of us, the killer seemed to just vanish. And that doesn't usually happen, not with serials."

"They have a cooling-off period," Samantha allowed as she thumbed through the documents. "But they don't usually go dormant for such an extended period."

"Then the girl taken now, Vanessa, we're all of similar ages at the times of our abductions.

From the same town but…" This was driving her crazy. Jill started to pace. "But I searched the federal databases and no one else matches the victim profile. Just the three of us. There weren't any abductions in nearby areas. It doesn't make sense, not unless—" She broke off.

"Unless what?" Samantha prompted.

Jill turned to look at the map she'd tacked on the wall. Her eyes narrowed as she studied it. "Unless he went much farther away. Unless the killer left town and was hunting in another area all these years." And maybe…just maybe those other girls hadn't been labeled as victims. "Runaways," Jill whispered as everything finally made sense for her. "It was staring me in the face the whole time, and I never even saw it."

"Jill?"

She looked back at Samantha. "When Vanessa's mother came in today, she didn't report her daughter as missing. She said Vanessa was a runaway." Her heart was pounding, her heart racing. "What if…what if everyone thought the others were runaways, too? What if *that* is his victim type? He's picking girls that people— their own families—would think had run away. That would make the parents slower to report the crimes, especially if they thought the kids would be back." *Only they never came home.* "And when the authorities were finally notified, the investigation process for a runaway is different than for a suspected child abduction. Time would be lost, clues never found..."

Victims just...gone.

Samantha stared at her in silence a moment, and then she said, "Would they have thought you were a runaway, too?"

Her hands had clenched into fists. "Both of my parents were dead. I'd been moved to a new town, a place that was totally foreign to me. I had no friends. No one close to me at all. My grandmother and I...things were strained between us at first. I was distant. Reserved." She swallowed. "Yes, I could have gone down as a runaway."

"And Christy Anderson?"

"Her family can tell us that for sure." But her instincts screamed...*yes*.

"Her family," Samantha repeated, her lips giving a wry twist. "That would be the brother currently in holding, right?"

Unfortunately, yes.

"I want to have a go at him," Samantha said.

Jill nodded. "I knew you would." Because the perps were Samantha's specialty. She never seemed to mind the darkness that cloaked the killers. Sometimes, Jill wondered if Samantha was drawn to that darkness.

"Will your sheriff give me the all clear to go in?" Samantha asked.

As if on cue, a light knock rapped against the office door. A moment later, the door opened, and Hayden slipped inside. "Jill, I need to talk to—" But he broke off when he glimpsed Samantha.

Jill realized her body was still too tense, her hands angry fists. She shook her head and tried to make herself relax. *I think I understand the perp now. I understand the victims.* "Hayden, this is my friend Agent Samantha Dark. And, Samantha, this is Sheriff Hayden Black."

Samantha offered Hayden her hand. "I have heard your name before…" she announced as her assessing gaze slid over him.

Hayden looked surprised. "You have?"

"Um." Samantha's face was expressionless, but her gaze had gone hard. "You're the man who—"

"I didn't save her," Hayden broke in quickly. "Look, if that's the story you heard. It's all wrong, okay? You want the truth? The truth is that Jill saved me that day. She pulled me back from a brink that no one else saw."

Samantha's head cocked to the right as her gaze slid over him, then slipped toward Jill. "Interesting. I was going to say…you were the man who broke Jill's heart."

Hayden's lips parted. His eyes jumped to Jill.

"But now…" Samantha nodded. "I see things are a lot more complex than I realized. Good. I like a nice mystery. Puzzles are my thing."

Hayden took a step toward Jill.

"I think I'll review these case files a bit." Samantha lifted the files. "I should also get a hotel room in town. Maybe something with an ocean view. Love the water…always reminds me of home." She headed for the door, and then she paused, glancing back. "Will I be able to talk to the prisoner?"

Hayden's gaze had narrowed as he glanced back her way.

"Jill can vouch for me," Samantha added, voice soft. "I assure you, I am very, very good at what I do. And if you want me to discover Kurt Anderson's secrets, then you'll let me have thirty minutes alone with him."

Then she was gone, easing from the room and shutting the door softly behind her.

Jill released a low breath. *Way to keep a confidence, Sam. I tell you one lousy truth during one drunken girls' night and this is the thanks I get—*

"Is she right?"

Jill turned away and raked a hand through her hair, being very, very careful not to touch her stitches. Her head was still throbbing. "She's the best profiler I know." Though to be honest, that wasn't Samantha's technical title at the FBI. She was on the fast track to be the lead agent in the Behavioral Analysis Unit. "Samantha knows how to slip into anyone's mind. It's a talent she—"

"Did I break your heart, Jill?" He'd closed the distance between them, and when he asked that question, his hand lifted and his fingers stroked her shoulder.

She tensed at his touch, and Jill thought about lying. But what would be the point? "Yes, but you knew that already." She turned to face him, tipping back her head as she stared up at him. "You were the center of my world back then. The person I loved far more than anyone else. And you—"

"I wasn't good enough for you."

"That is such utter bull, Hayden."

"Whispers had followed me my whole life. Would I be like my old man? When would I get thrown in jail? I'd never amount to anything, then you met me on a pier. And after that day, everyone looked at me differently."

"Hayden…"

"People said I was a hero, but they were wrong."

No, he had—

"I followed that vehicle because I couldn't let you go. You looked at me in a way no one ever had before. You looked at me…" He swallowed. "And I changed. I liked the way I looked in your eyes. But I was holding you too tightly. I could see it. Hell, most people in the town did. You were becoming my obsession, and that wasn't right. You needed *more*."

"You dreamed of joining the FBI. Of making a difference. I wanted you to have that dream, Jill. I wanted to prove that I could be more than a selfish bastard with you. So I stepped back. I wasn't going to *hold* you back. I gave up the thing that was the most important in my life. Then I joined the military. I wanted to prove that I *could* be someone you'd be proud of. That I could protect and defend and that I could—"

"Stop." The word emerged, low, angry. "Just… *stop*."

He stared down at her. Jill's breath sawed from her lungs. "I was always proud of you. You should have seen that. I always wanted to be with you. You should have seen that, too." She pressed her lips together and felt the pain of the past once more. Only once…*because I don't want the past any longer*. "But we were two kids, Hayden. Two kids who'd clung too tightly to each other for so long. We were both making mistakes. Both stumbling along. That was then. We aren't those kids any longer."

"You're right." He nodded. "We're not. And I'll be damned if I make the same mistake again."

"Hayden?"

He pulled her even closer. "I love you."

Jill shook her head.

"I love you. If you hadn't come to Hope, I was coming to Atlanta to find you. I wanted another chance with you. I wanted to be with you. Taking the job as sheriff, joining the navy, damn it, don't you see? It was all for you. To show you that I could be the man you needed. That I am better. I am—"

Jill fisted her hand in his shirt and jerked him down toward her. She kissed him. Deep and wild and crazy. She didn't hold back her desire or the emotions that seemed to be ripping her apart. She just let go...the way she'd always wanted.

His arms closed around her. The heat of his body surrounded her. So close. So strong. So very Hayden.

His mouth lifted, just a bit and he growled, "When this case is over, I want another chance with you."

Her eyes were closed. She wanted to sink into him and escape the pain all around, but that wasn't an option. Christy needed them. "When this case is over..."

She made her eyes open. She stared at him. His hard, determined face. So handsome.

"I want another chance with you, too," Jill whispered. Because she wouldn't be afraid. And she wouldn't let doubts hold her back. Hayden was the man she wanted.

Hayden was the man she'd have.

"THIRTY MINUTES."

Samantha nodded as she stared up at Hayden Black. He certainly wasn't the guy she'd anticipated. When Jill had talked about Hayden, well, Samantha had pictured a stuffy guy, reserved, strong but...controlled.

This man wasn't controlled. His emotions seemed to spill from him, and, every single time that he glanced at Jill...

Jill wasn't the only one with a broken heart.

Hayden Black was strong, dangerous and, judging by the way he walked, that careful stride of his—

"You're profiling me, aren't you?" Hayden asked as he stilled in front of the heavy door that would take them back to the holding cell.

Samantha gave a quick, slightly nervous laugh. "Sorry. I tend to have trouble turning that off." And she knew it unnerved people. "My bad. Occupational hazard."

He faced her, crossed his arms over his chest and waited.

He was a sexy guy, she could see where Jill would have been attracted to the man but—

"Are you going to fill me in?" Hayden prompted.

"Excuse me?"

"I want to know what you think. Who am I?"

Uh… "Here? Now?" She wanted to get back into holding and take a go at Anderson. But, fine, if this was the price of admission. "I already knew you were ex-military, but I'm betting you were the leader of your team. You're too used to giving orders otherwise. You walk into a room and immediately access every threat, every weakness there. You thrive on risk, you love the rush of adrenaline. You're dangerous—"

His jaw hardened. "Dangerous?"

"Oh, yes." She believed that completely. She was staring into the eyes of a man who wouldn't hesitate to kill. Who probably *hadn't*. When you took a life, it left a mark on you, not outside, but deep within. Hayden carried that mark.

So did she.

"You think I'm dangerous to Jill?" His eyes had gone cold and hard.

But Samantha shook her head. "Not to her. I think she's probably the safest woman on the planet when you're near." Kind of like Lois Lane. "I think you'd do anything for her, but if some fool tries to take her from you again—"

"That *won't* happen."

She saw plenty when she looked at him. "Tried to live without her, huh? Tried to do the right thing?"

He lifted one blond brow.

"Bet that sucked." Samantha smiled. "Guess you won't be making that same mistake again."

"I'm surprised you're not telling me to stay the hell away from her."

"Why? Because you're so big and bad?" She laughed. "Jill can handle big and bad. What she *can't* handle is losing you again. Maybe you should ask her about her contacts at the CIA. Ask what she found so very fascinating about a certain SEAL team. Even when you weren't with her, trust me, she kept you close."

His eyes widened the faintest bit. Nice eyes. Dark. Deep. And the way he looked at Jill with those eyes…as if she were the center of his world.

Because she is.

For an instant, Samantha felt a brush of sadness. It would be nice to be looked at that way. To be cared about, in that way.

She cleared her throat. "So, look, as fun as profiling you is…you aren't the killer I'm after." And she chose her words with deliberate care. "So if you're still up to giving me that thirty minutes with Anderson…"

"I am." He motioned toward the door. "My deputy Finn Patrick will stay with you during the session. Jill and I are going to conduct some more sweeps of the beaches."

"Jill should call it a night," Samantha muttered. The woman had looked dead on her feet. An up-close brush with a bomb would do that.

"She doesn't want to leave Vanessa out there alone. Jill thinks we're working against a clock. Twenty-four hours and then, well, that *then* part can't happen."

No, it couldn't.

He opened the door that led back to holding. She brushed by him and saw that a deputy was already back there, waiting on her. *Deputy Finn, I presume.* But she hesitated and glanced back at Hayden. "Stay close to Jill." Because while she'd been reading the files, alarm bells had gone off in her head. She was missing something with this case. They all were. She knew it…

What?

"Always." He gave her a little salute and turned away.

She marched deeper into the holding area. A man sat with hunched shoulders on a cot inside that cell. He glanced up at her. "My lawyer said for me not to speak with another soul here, so, lady, you should just turn around and keep walking right back out."

She did keep walking. Not out, though, but all the way up to his cell. Her high heels clicked on the floor.

His frown deepened. "Lady…"

"We can get your lawyer in here," Samantha said because she knew just how this game worked. "He can listen to my interview with you. He can tell you what to say or what not to say. We can do all of that."

His gaze slid over her. "Who are you?"

"Samantha Dark." The name would mean nothing to him. She had her FBI badge clipped to her hip but he wasn't looking away from her face. He was staring directly at her, gazing into her eyes as if he had nothing to hide.

Such a lie. We all have plenty to hide. Too much.

"We can certainly go that route," Samantha continued. "But then, another girl will probably die. A girl just like Christy."

He flinched.

"Do you really want that to happen? Do you want another death on you?"

"I didn't kill my sister!"

And that was why he would talk to her. He couldn't talk to Jillian…when he looked at her, Samantha knew the past overwhelmed Kurt Anderson. Guilt tore at his insides. When he looked at Hayden Black, shame filled him. *Be-*

cause Hayden saved Jill but you couldn't save your sister.

This guy carried his grief like a cloak around him. Time to rip that cloak away. "You didn't kill her." She nodded. "So how about we find out who did?"

Chapter Thirteen

The full moon hung heavy in the sky as it shone down on the waves. The roar of the water was so loud, too loud, as it beat against the shore.

Searchers were sweeping the entire city. Deputies, volunteers, anyone and everyone. Jill knew that Hayden had already checked all the vacant and vacation rental properties in the area.

There had been no sign of Vanessa.

But, that morning… *It had all started on this beach.* Vanessa had been there. Her bike had been removed from the parking lot, taken in as evidence, but…

You were here, Vanessa. This is where everything started for you. Where would it end?

She looked to the left and saw Hayden patrolling. His flashlight swept over the beach. She knew what he feared, just as she knew why he'd wanted them to start beach searches immediately.

Christy Anderson's body had been left on the beach.

Hayden thought they'd find Vanessa's body discarded in the same way. Every minute that passed...*he thinks it is a minute that brings us closer to her death.*

Her grip tightened on the flashlight that she carried. There were no bodies to find, not yet. "He's still here." The words pulled from her.

Hayden was so far away, she didn't think he'd heard her, but he moved closer. He was a big, dark shadow in the night.

"He's still here," Jill said again, her voice stronger, harder. "There's something about this town. I think it's always pulled him back."

"Or maybe he just never left." Hayden's light pointed at the sand near her feet. "You and I did, but maybe he didn't. Maybe all of these years, he was right here."

A killer, hiding in their midst.

"Do you think Vanessa is still alive?" Hayden asked quietly.

She considered that for a moment. Not what she wanted to believe but the truth. *Was she still alive?* "Yes." And that was something they could use. "Because he doesn't have what he wants. Not yet."

"He wants you."

"No." Because that wasn't exactly the truth. "He wants me dead."

"JILLIAN WEST HAS a new theory about the victims," Samantha said. She stood a few inches away from the bars, her gaze on the man who'd risen to stare at her. "She thinks the perp picked girls who would have initially been labeled as runaways, not abduction victims. A smart move because that would have bought the perp more time to cover his tracks."

Kurt's brow furrowed.

"Would your sister have run away?"

"No, no, Christy *wouldn't*—"

"Your parents are divorced," Samantha interrupted. A deliberate tactic. *Never start with the question you really want answered. Trick, lead, catch your suspect off guard.*

"Yeah. My mom couldn't take it after—after Christy. My dad was drinking all the time. Hardly the same man…she had to get away."

"And she took you with her."

His brows notched up, running toward his forehead. "Yeah, so?"

She just stared.

"You think I abandoned him? Is that it? Look, lady, I didn't have a choice. I didn't—"

"I don't think you abandoned him. But I do wonder, were there any problems between your parents *before* Christy's death?"

"My dad…he worked a lot, okay? He traveled all the time. He wasn't there much, that was my mom's complaint. That he was always on the road."

She blinked. "What kind of work did your father do back then?"

"Pharmaceutical sales."

Samantha didn't let her expression alter.

"He had a territory to cover. So he wasn't at home a lot. He was providing for us. Doing the best he could." He raked a hand through his hair. "He just…he lost it after my sister died. Drinking…drinking so much and yelling all the time. Always blaming—" But he broke off, clamping his lips shut.

"Always blaming you?" Samantha finished. "Your mom?"

He gave a bitter laugh. "No. Always blaming Jill. Always saying it was her fault." He turned on his heel. "Dad used to rage about her, over and over. Saying if she'd died, Christy would be alive. That it was always Jill's fault. Even when he got fired from his job—for all the damn drinking—that was still Jill's fault."

"But Jill was a victim," she said carefully. "You understand that, don't you? Jill didn't hurt your sister. Someone else did that. Someone else took her. Someone else broke her neck. Someone else put her on that beach. Covered her up…"

His head sagged. "Christy always liked the

beach. She'd go out there for hours and just watch the waves. She loved that place."

Christy was covered. She was taken to a place she loved. Samantha thought of the crime scene photos that she'd glimpsed in the old file.

Christy's clothes had been perfectly arranged. No sexual assault. She cleared her throat. "Tell me about the last time you saw Christy."

He glanced back at her, frowning.

She'd deliberately switched her questions because Samantha was about to loop the knot.

So to speak.

"What was your sister doing, the last time you saw her?"

He rubbed his hand over the back of his neck. "She was looking for our dad. She came to my room right after she'd gotten home from her softball practice, asking where he was. She wanted to go out with some of her friends but she wanted money to spend, so she was looking for Dad." His shoulders rolled back. "I was leaving so I barely even said three words to her as I walked down the hall. I didn't have time for Christy. Too cool, you know? Too damn cool."

"What were those three words?"

He blinked at her.

"Do you remember those three words?" Samantha pushed.

He swallowed. "Yeah, yeah, I remember them."

Samantha waited.

"Dad's out back." He gave a grating laugh. "That's all I said. 'Dad's out back.' Hardly anything earth-shattering, right? Not like that is gonna break her case wide-open."

Before she could reply, the door to the holding room opened behind her. Deputy Finn Patrick rushed from his position to intercept the redheaded guy in the crisp gray suit who'd just stepped in as if he owned the place.

"Why is my client being interviewed?" The redheaded man pulled a folded white piece of paper from his suit pocket.

Another deputy was behind the lawyer—a woman with short-cropped brown hair. Samantha had met her earlier, Deputy Wendy Hollow. Wendy appeared none too pleased as she shared a fast glance with Finn. "Judge Eisen just called. We've got orders to release Anderson."

"Of course, you do," the lawyer retorted, voice saccharine sweet. "After all, at least one person in this town—a person in a position of power—realizes that the Anderson family has been through enough hell. My client is a victim here. Some twisted individual—the same individual who killed his sister—is tormenting him the same way that perpetrator is tormenting Special Agent West. A tragedy, all the way around." He nodded toward Finn. "My client needs to be processed so he can get the hell out of here. It's late. He needs to get home. After all, he has to take care of his father."

Samantha glanced back at Kurt. She wasn't done with him.

"I'm sorry," the lawyer murmured as he slipped closer to her. "But *who* are you? And why were you talking *alone* with my client?"

She turned her head and gave him her own saccharine smile. She was pretty good at that. "I'm not alone. Deputy Patrick was with us."

His gaze raked over her and lingered on the badge. "FBI? If my client's rights were violated—"

"I wanted to talk to her," Kurt suddenly called out.

His lawyer's eyes widened in surprise. Samantha made sure not to let her surprise show. Another trick she had—she only let her emotions out when she wanted others to see them. Most days, she knew it was better to *not* let anyone see her weakness.

Killers enjoyed weakness far too much. When they saw weakness, it was like a shark scenting blood in the water.

"I want to find Christy's killer. I want to stop him," Kurt stated flatly. "But I don't know anything that can help. I let my sister down years ago, and I'm still letting her down now."

HAYDEN'S PHONE RANG, a jarring cry in the dark. He swore and pulled the phone from his pocket, glancing at the screen. It was a new phone, one that he'd picked up just a few hours before. *Since his last one basically melted.* "It's Finn," he said. "Better take this." He turned from her, pacing a few feet away.

Her body stiffened as she watched him. *Don't let Vanessa's body have been discovered. Don't—*

"Judge Eisen did what?" Hayden exploded. "No, no, that guy is way overstepping his authority. Doesn't he realize the magnitude of this case? To let Kurt Anderson just walk—"

Her phone rang. She pulled it out, frowning. The screen had been smashed to hell and back at the bomb scene, and she was lucky the thing hadn't melted on her, like Hayden's had.

When Jill saw the name on the screen, her heart seemed to stop. Unknown Caller. She swiped her finger over that cracked screen, trying to make sure she didn't slice her skin and she slipped away from Hayden, hunching her shoulders. "Agent West."

"Were you afraid, when the fire came for you?"

"No, I was angry." She kept her voice low. Behind her, she could still hear Hayden blasting at Finn. "I thought we'd agreed to a trade."

"Um, but you cheated. You had a trace on

the phone." He paused. "Bet you still have one going."

I bet I do. Uncovering an unknown caller's telephone number was actually an easy business. A simple reverse phone lookup revealed that information. But actually tracking the mystery caller's signal, *finding* that phone…it took more work. *And help from the FBI.*

"Here I went to all the trouble of getting a new burner phone…" He gave a rough laugh. "And you're still playing your same game."

"Sorry to put you out," she snapped.

His laughter had died away. "If you send all the deputies and your FBI buddies swarming on me, I promise you, Vanessa Gray will die."

That was the first official confirmation that he'd taken Vanessa. *Right from this beach. The same place, the same way.* "How do I know she isn't already dead?"

There was a beat of silence. "H-hello?" A girl's voice, weak and raspy.

"Vanessa?"

"I—I want my brother," the girl whispered. "Can I please get—" But her voice was abruptly cut off.

Each breath that Jill took seemed to chill her lungs.

"She's alive," the man rasped at her. "But how long she stays that way, well, it depends on you."

Jill looked over her shoulder. Hayden was pacing as he talked, but he was glancing her way. She started to signal to him—

"Don't." One word, growled.

And she knew the caller was close enough to watch her. *He's close and he has Vanessa with him.*

"I don't want Hayden Black getting involved. I don't want deputies. I don't want anyone but you."

She swallowed. "You still offering an exchange? Me for Vanessa?" She kept her voice as low as possible.

"Yes."

"Like I'm supposed to trust you?" Hell, no. "You just want to lead me into another cabin so that you can blow me to pieces."

"That is one option."

Her hold tightened on the phone.

"I could always kill Vanessa right now," he said. "Since you're so untrusting of me… I could snap her neck right—"

Vanessa was screaming in the background. Begging.

"Don't," Jill said. "Just…*don't.*"

Silence.

"Give me the second option," she ordered.

But he didn't speak.

"Damn it—"

"It's your fault she's dead," he said, his voice different, aching. "I never meant…you did all this. You ruined everything. Destroyed the life I had. It was all so perfect before you."

He wasn't talking about Vanessa. She knew he meant Christy. *It's your fault she's dead.* "Another young girl doesn't have to die," Jill said softly. "We can end this. Tell me where to be and I'll come." With backup. With guns blazing. With enough strength to take him out and to save Vanessa.

"That's not how it works." Just like that, the emotion was gone from his raspy voice as if he'd just flipped a switch inside of himself. "Get rid of Hayden. Go back to your house on the beach. When I'm sure you're alone, I'll call you." A brief pause. "If you use the FBI to track this call, I'll know. I'll be watching. I'll see them come and she'll be dead before anyone breaches the door."

The line ended. Jill stared at her phone.

"No, no, Finn, just let the guy go, all right? But I want a tail on him. You make sure that a deputy is watching Anderson 24/7. Right. Yes, yes, I'm on my way."

She pushed her phone into her pocket and took a bracing breath. She turned to see Hayden end his call.

"Kurt Anderson is walking," he said, striding

toward her. "Looks like we don't have enough evidence to hold him. All circumstantial. So he's leaving the station now."

So...if he was at the station, with eyes on him, then Kurt Anderson wasn't her twisted caller. His story had been real. Someone had taken his car to try and frame him. Someone who'd been able to get easy access to the Anderson house.

"I heard you talking, too," Hayden said. "What's happening? What's going on?"

Get rid of Hayden. She looked over his shoulder. In the distance, she saw a line of beach houses, with cheery lights glowing from their interiors. Beacons shining to her. The caller had been watching. He was *still* watching. Jill knew that.

She also knew...*if I follow his rules, Vanessa will live.*

The perp had made this a very, very personal battle. It wasn't about abducting victims to him. It was about getting back at Jill. Punishing her.

"I was getting the same news," she murmured, still looking off in the distance. "But I don't think Kurt Anderson is our guy. We need to be focusing elsewhere. I mean, he was too young to be the man who took me years ago."

"Yeah, but that doesn't mean he isn't the SOB who broke into your cabin or who set the bomb for you. He and his old man… Jill, they have a lot of fury in them. A lot of hate. And it seems to be directed right at you."

Just as the caller's fury was directed at her.

It's your fault she's dead.

"Yes," Jill said softly. "It is. It's all on me." Because she'd gotten away. She'd lived, but another had died in her place.

"I need to get back to the station."

Yes, that was exactly where she needed him to be.

His hand curled under her chin. "I know you want to keep searching, but there isn't anything out here for us."

Wrong. *He* was out there. The perp. The man who'd taken Vanessa. "She's so scared, Hayden." The words slipped from her. "She wants to come home. She wants her brother."

"I know her brother," he said, his thumb sliding tenderly along her jaw. "I served with him. Porter is a good man. I already put out a call through my contacts to get him back here. He's Black Ops right now, but I'm doing my best to get him home."

And she didn't want that man to return home only to bury his sister.

"We'll resume the search at first light. That's when the rest of your team is arriving, right?"

Yes, she'd called in the southeastern CARD team for backup.

"More boots on the ground," Hayden said. "We *will* find Vanessa."

She leaned up on her toes and pressed her lips to his. He seemed startled by her fast move, but she'd needed to kiss him once more. To taste him. To just remember what it was like to be safe and loved.

By him.

With him.

The wind blew against her and he was so strong and steady. Her haven.

His tongue slid against her lips, thrust into her mouth. Desire flared hot in her blood. His kiss, his touch…that was all it took. She wanted him. Needed him.

But now wasn't the time to have him. She savored Hayden just a moment longer. Then she eased away from him. For a moment, she just stared at him in the darkness. Her Hayden. She swallowed and asked, "Take me back to my cabin?"

He gazed down at her, his eyes gleaming.

"My head…it's hurting a bit. I think I need to rest some so I can be sharp for the search in the morning."

Hayden nodded. "Of course." He took a step back but seemed to study her.

She exhaled slowly. "Thank you." She'd get him to leave her at the cabin and then…

Then the real fight will begin.

SAMANTHA TAPPED HER fingers on the check-in desk at the sheriff's office as she watched the lawyer hustle Kurt Anderson out of that place. Kurt looked tired, his shoulders slumped and…

His gaze darted back toward her.

That man looks guilty. Every time he glanced her way, she saw the taint of guilt in his stare.

"Sheriff said for me to send a tail with him," Finn murmured as he sidled up next to her. "I'm gonna be that tail."

Her gaze slid toward him.

"I'll make sure the guy doesn't hurt anyone. And if he does anything suspicious, if he can lead us to that missing girl, I'll be calling Sheriff Black right away."

She slipped him her card. "Make sure you keep me updated, too."

He blinked.

But before he could say more, Kurt's lawyer was opening the door and the guy was waltzing out with their number one suspect.

"Showtime for you, Deputy." Samantha inclined her head toward the door.

Finn waited a moment, probably trying not to

look too obvious, and then he slipped out after the others.

Samantha exhaled. She didn't think Kurt was their perp, but things sure weren't adding up for her.

Dad's out back. She grabbed the file that Jill had prepared on Christy Anderson's disappearance, and she flipped back through the witness testimony. Theodore Anderson had been questioned about his whereabouts at the time of his daughter's disappearance. According to him, he'd been out on a solo fishing trip. He'd left late the night before and hadn't gotten back until midday...long after his daughter had been taken.

But why did Kurt say his dad was out back if the guy was actually out fishing?

Had Kurt been lying to her? Or had his father lied to the authorities years before?

Samantha nodded to Deputy Hollow—Wendy had taken over the check-in desk—and then she hurried outside. She needed to find Jill and talk to her more about that old case. Maybe Jill remembered details that could help her. She grabbed for her keys and hit the button to unlock her rental car. Her heels clicked on the pavement and the roar of the ocean filled her ears.

A sudden awareness had her tensing. A shiver slid down her spine and Samantha knew that she wasn't alone.

She looked to the left—the lawyer and Kurt Anderson were gone. Finn's patrol car was slipping from the lot.

Her gaze slid to the right—and to the man who was walking away from the shadows.

"There you are," he said, his voice deep and rumbling. His stride was determined as he stalked toward her. "Want to tell me what the hell you are doing?"

Her brows lifted.

"Partners don't just cut out of town without any word," he added darkly. The light from the station fell on his face. And her new partner at the FBI—Blake Gamble—sure didn't look happy with her. "If you're working a case, *we're* working it. You don't get to leave me in the dust."

What in the hell is he doing here? "How did you know where I was? And *why* are you here?"

"The director sent me down. Said I should be with you, even if it isn't an 'official' investigation for us."

It was official as far as she was concerned. "I was called in as a favor," she said, turning to face him fully. Blake was a big guy, well over six feet, and built along the same hard, tough lines as Jill's Sheriff Black. "I'm here for a friend."

He stopped walking when he was less than a foot away from her. "And you didn't think I'd agree to help out your *friend*?"

She was still trying to feel out her new relationship with Blake. So far, the guy seemed to be a definite by-the-book type. But she had a feeling Blake had lots of layers hidden beneath his careful control. "I wasn't sure what you'd do."

"Well, let me tell you… I'd have your back." The words were simple. Easy.

"That's what partners do, right?" Blake continued. "We watch out for each other?"

"Yes." That's what they were supposed to do.

"Besides, I know Jillian West, too. Not as well as you do, but I would never walk away from a case *or* from my partner. So tell me what I can do to help." He gave a decisive nod. "Because the boss said there was a missing kid in this town. What can we do to bring her home?"

Chapter Fourteen

"Seriously, Hayden, you don't have to walk me up." Jill had opened her door and the car's interior light spilled down on her. "I've got this."

He locked his jaw and forced a nod. He wanted to go up there, do a full search and make sure the place was safe…*because it's Jill.* But the woman was armed. She knew how to spot the signs of an intruder, and—

Hell, I just don't want to leave her.

"I'll check in at the station and be back," he assured her.

She climbed from the car. "You don't have to do that."

He jumped out and followed her, catching her arm before she could head for the stairs that would take her up to the main level of the cabin. "I want to do that." Didn't she get that? He wanted to spend his days and nights with her. They'd talked about a second chance, and he wasn't going to let that chance get away. For him, Jill was it. His everything. His one shot at happiness. He wouldn't lose her again. "I'll check in, then I'll be back." But as he stared at her, worry gnawed at him. "Hell, I'll just stay here." The woman had a concussion after all, damn it. "You might need me and I—"

"I need some time alone, Hayden." Her gaze was on the waves, not him. "Just…give me tonight, would you? I don't need you to keep guard over me. I can protect myself, and I need that time."

You're pushing her too hard. He looked down at his hand. "Right." Hayden made himself let her go. "I'll send a patrol by to—"

"Always the protector, aren't you? Even when I don't want protecting."

He was missing something. She wasn't looking at him and her voice seemed too calm. Too reserved.

"I need this night on my own. If it makes you feel better to send a patrol circling by later, then do it. But I'd rather every available unit you have… I'd rather your efforts be focused on Vanessa and not me." Now her gaze finally did come back to him. "She's what matters now. You understand that, don't you?"

"Jill—"

She backed away from him. "If I see any trouble, you'll be the first one I call."

This wasn't right. The scene was wrong. *She* was wrong.

"Good night, Hayden." Jill turned away. She hurried up the stairs and didn't glance back at him. He stood there a moment, watching until she disappeared inside. The lights flashed on in her cabin.

He still didn't leave. Something was wrong. Something was nagging at him. She'd kissed him so frantically on the beach...

And now she's sending me packing.

He lingered for a moment longer, then headed back to his patrol car. He slipped inside and a few moments later, he was heading away from Jill and her cabin by the shore.

He glanced in his rearview mirror, but Hayden only saw darkness.

I'll be back tonight, Jill. Whether you want me here or not. I'll be back. Because finding Vanessa Gray was absolutely a priority for him. But keeping Jill safe?

That is always my first mission.

JILL HELD HER BREATH as she stared below and watched Hayden's car slowly pull away. He'd been suspicious at the end, and she hadn't been sure that he'd leave her alone.

She hadn't wanted him to go. She'd wanted to pull him in, to get him to help her stop the perp out there. *But he was watching.* And if Vanessa's abductor saw her rush in with Hayden at her side, then an innocent girl could die.

She put her phone down on the kitchen table. She stared at it a moment, willing the thing to ring. It didn't.

So she moved back. She went into her bedroom, and opened her suitcase. Jill took out her backup weapon and she strapped it to her ankle. Then she checked her service gun. Its weight was reassuring in her hand. She might be playing by the perp's rules, but she didn't intend to make herself easy prey.

No, when morning came, Jill intended to still be standing.

And Vanessa Gray would be at her side. *Alive.* Safe. She wouldn't lose another victim. She *couldn't* lose her.

Her phone rang, jerking her attention and Jill rushed back into the den. Her phone was shaking on the table, vibrating. She peered down at the broken screen.

Unknown Caller.

SHE JUST WANTS her brother.

Hayden slammed on the brakes. The car's tires screeched.

Jill's words had been replaying in his head as he tried to figure out why she'd withdrawn from him. Back at the beach, she'd been talking about Vanessa. About the girl being afraid.

And Jill had said that Vanessa wanted her brother.

Maybe she'd just been talking, piecing together parts of Vanessa's life and assuming that the girl would be afraid and wanting the security of having her brother close. After all, Jill had talked to Vanessa's mother. She'd known that Vanessa had an older brother who was currently out of the country.

Maybe she'd been making a victim profile.

He spun the car around and shoved his foot down on the gas.

Or maybe Jill had been repeating what she'd heard Vanessa say. Her voice had softened when she spoke on the beach. There'd been pain whispering in her words...

And then Jill had wanted to go home. Alone.

Sonofa—

He used his Bluetooth connection to call the sheriff's office. When his call was answered, he demanded, "I want to talk to Samantha Dark—is she still there?"

"No, Sheriff," Wendy answered. "She left a few moments ago."

Hell. "Do you know if she called Jill West before she left? Did Agent Dark make *any* phone calls while she was at the station?"

"I don't know, sir. Sorry."

"If you see her again, get her to call me. Right the hell away." He ended the connection and narrowed his eyes on the road up ahead. If Samantha hadn't been on the phone with Jill…then Jill could have been talking to the perp again. The guy had called her once, offering up a deal, maybe he'd called again.

But Jill would have told me. She would have—

He was near Jill's cabin. Close enough that he saw her car. Saw *her* heading to that car.

Hayden killed the lights on his own vehicle. Jill was moving fast as she spun her car out and left the beach. She'd had her phone to her ear. She'd been talking frantically to someone.

To the perp?

Jill would lie to me…if it meant that she could help a victim.

The killer had offered Jill a trade once before. Hayden was very afraid that the guy had made her another deal.

Her voice slipped through his mind. *She's what matters now. You understand that, don't you?*

She'd been telling him, right then, and Hayden hadn't picked up on the truth. As her car headed down the narrow road, he didn't even hesitate.

Hayden had followed Jill once before, followed her on a dark and desperate path, and he'd damn well do it again.

He'd follow Jill anywhere, even straight to hell, if that was what it took. He kept his lights off and he didn't go too fast. He didn't want Jill to see him. Jill...or the perp. *He could be watching.*

Whatever twisted plans that jerk had, they weren't going to happen.

You aren't getting her, bastard. I'll do whatever it takes, but I won't lose Jill again.

"IT'S THE NORMAL houses that hide the worst monsters," Samantha said as she slammed her car door and stared up at the house located at 1509 Sea Breeze Way. "They always look so innocent and then—too late—you see that facade was just a lie."

Blake hurried around the front of the car and came to her side. "So...we're going to interrogate the guy? Right now? In the middle of the night?"

"Not an interrogation. Just one follow-up question." She patted his chest and tried not to notice that the guy was seriously muscled. He was her partner. *Only* her partner. There was no mixing business with pleasure at the FBI, no matter how handsome she might find Blake to be. "And it's not as if the guy is asleep. He just got released a little while ago. His lawyer dropped him off and Kurt's in there, probably pacing the floors." She inclined her head toward the house that waited—with seemingly all of its interior lights turned on.

"As long as he doesn't go screaming to his lawyer about FBI harassment..." Blake muttered.

"He won't." She was sure of this. "Because something else is going on here." Something that Kurt knew but wasn't sharing, something that seemed to be tearing him apart. She glanced down the street, and, sure enough, sitting three houses back, underneath the heavy shelter of an oak tree's limbs, she saw Deputy Finn waiting in his patrol car.

It was good to know the sheriff's office was keeping watch on the Anderson house. Especially because that perfectly trimmed, perfectly normal house felt wrong to her.

Nothing is ever as perfect as it seems. Her friend Cameron Latham would have said that bit. Like her, Cameron had gotten his PhD in criminal psychology from Harvard. Cameron was her sounding board, whenever she had a particularly good—or bad—theory swirling in her head, she'd run her thoughts by him. Cameron would take one look at that little house and say, *Too perfect, Sam. Find the lies inside.*

That was just what she was there to do.

Samantha lifted her chin and led the way up the carefully trimmed lawn. She reached the door and rapped against the wood. She heard fumbling inside, the shuffle of footsteps, the hum of a TV and then—

The door opened soundlessly. No little creaks, no groans of the hinges. *Perfect.*

Kurt Anderson stood in the doorway, and he looked far, far from perfect. His hair stood on end, as if he'd been raking his fingers through it. His face was pale, his gaze desperate.

"Mr. Anderson?" Samantha tried a quick smile. "Our conversation was interrupted earlier…" *Conversation, interrogation—whatever you want to call it.* "I just had one question for you."

"He's not here."

Samantha frowned at that abrupt response. "Um, who isn't here?"

"My dad." Kurt's hand raked through his hair. "Knew this would happen… I was gone too long… He'd been so good…so good, but to mess up now…"

She didn't look back at Blake, but she could practically feel her partner's sudden tension. "Mess up what, exactly?"

Kurt's hand fell. "He's been sober for a year and seven months, ever since I came back to town. I *made* him get sober. But me being taken to the station… Jill pushing about Christy… opening up the past, I know it's pushed him over the edge. I found a whiskey bottle in the kitchen." He swallowed, his Adam's apple bobbing. "It's empty."

"May I come inside?" Samantha asked him, her voice soft.

Kurt stumbled back. "He's gone. I need… I need Hayden to put out an APB for him. My dad isn't the same when he drinks. He could get hurt." If possible, Kurt's skin turned even paler. "He could…hurt someone else."

The inside of the home was in shambles. The couch had been turned over, a lamp was smashed and a picture frame… Samantha bent to pick up the frame from the floor, and shards of glass dropped near her feet. She stared at the picture of the smiling girl with blond hair and dimples. The same girl who had been in the old file at the police station. A picture of Christy Anderson, standing with her father.

"Did you do this?" Blake's deep voice rumbled from behind her.

"This?" Kurt appeared confused, and then he glanced around the room. "No, no. Dad must have done it. I told you, when he drinks, he's not the same. He gets so angry, like a different person. But he was sober until Jill came back."

His hands fisted. "She should have stayed away. He saw her the first day she was back in town, saw her and Hayden and everything came rushing back for him. Like a ticking bomb… I could see it happening."

A ticking bomb…pretty interesting description considering what had happened to Jill and Hayden.

"Wait. Who the hell are you?" Kurt suddenly demanded as his gaze sharpened on Blake.

Samantha kept her grip on the picture frame. "He's my partner, Blake Gamble. I told you, we had one more question for you."

"Forget your damn questions!" Kurt yelled. "Get Hayden on the line! Make him go look for my father! Get the guy out here, now!"

"I will," Samantha assured him. "I'll get a whole team to look for your father."

Kurt nodded, appearing a bit appeased.

"But I just need you to answer one question for me first. Just one."

"Lady," Kurt growled as he took an aggressive step toward her. "You aren't playing with my dad's life."

Blake was suddenly at her side. "Watch the tone, buddy. *Watch* it."

Her chin notched up as she met Kurt's blazing stare. "I'm not playing any game. I'm just trying to find out the truth." A very long overdue truth.

"The day your sister disappeared, your father said he was out fishing. But tonight at the station, you told me that he was home, that you'd told Christy your father was out back."

Kurt licked his lips.

"What's the truth, Kurt? Just tell me that. Where was your father when Christy vanished?"

JILL PARKED HER car near the pier. She sat behind the wheel for a moment, her hands gripping the steering wheel. And the phone beside her rang again.

Her hand flew out and her finger swept over that fractured screen.

"I can see you, Jill. And you came alone. Just as you said."

She was so tired of the grating voice. So tired of the games.

"Go to the end of the pier...and then jump in the water," he ordered her.

"Are you insane? Why would I—"

"Swim straight out, and you'll find my boat."

Jill sucked in a sharp breath. *He's on a boat. No wonder he was able to see me when I was on the beach with Hayden earlier. The guy was watching us from the water.* Probably using night vision binoculars.

And the man who'd broken into her cabin...

they'd found his motorcycle but not him. *Why? Because he'd swum out to his boat?*

"I can see you perfectly, Jill. I'll watch you swim to me. Just you. If I spot another car coming with you, if I spot any deputies or the damn sheriff, then I'll break Vanessa's throat and throw her body in the water."

"I'm by myself. You don't have to worry."

"That's what I thought before, too. That I had you all alone, and *he* was there."

Jill checked her weapons. She hadn't counted on a dive in the water. The guns might not even shoot when she came out.

So I need another weapon. Something else I can use.

"Walk on the pier, Jill. Get in the water. *Now.* You have fifteen minutes to reach me. Fifteen minutes or Vanessa dies."

She hung up on him. Then she sent a text, fast and frantically. She opened her glove box and grabbed the screwdriver that was inside. Not much of a weapon, but it was one that water wouldn't destroy. She shoved the screwdriver inside the top of her jeans, hoping to keep it secured in place, and then Jill climbed out of the car. Her steps were quick as she headed out onto the pier. The moon shone down on her, giving Jill plenty of light as she hurried across the wood. She looked out at the water, but didn't see any lights from boats.

He's got his lights off because he doesn't want to be seen. He's out there, waiting. No cabin by the marsh needed for him this time.

How perfect was a boat for this type of crime? He could take his victims, kill them, dump the bodies. If he weighed them down, they might not be discovered at all.

The victims would just stay missing.

She reached the end of the pier and stared out into the darkness. For just a moment, she remembered a blond boy standing in that spot. Hair a little too long. Eyes so dark and deep.

Hayden. I love you.

She hoped he knew that. She'd never stopped loving him. She didn't think she could.

Jill exhaled slowly and climbed over the wooden railing of the pier. She sat there a moment, staring at the waves. And then...

She jumped.

HE DIDN'T PULL into the pier's parking lot. When Hayden saw Jill turn up ahead of him, he braked his car, killed the engine and left it just off the road. Then he kept to the shadows as he hurried toward the pier. He arrived just as Jill started walking down that long wooden pier. She was looking straight ahead, staring out over the water.

His eyes narrowed as he scanned the area. There was no one else there. Jill couldn't possibly be meeting the perp...*he wasn't here.*

Or maybe, maybe the guy just hadn't arrived yet. Maybe Jill was supposed to meet the kidnapper. An exchange? Was that about to happen? Jill trading her life for Vanessa's? He could see her trying to do some move like that. Hell, he and Jill needed to have a serious damn talk. She couldn't keep risking herself like this.

He trailed behind her, but he never went into the moonlight. He stopped near the old souvenir shop. He could see Jill perfectly as she walked forward, never hesitating. And then...

His phone vibrated in his pocket. He pulled it out quickly but didn't look at the text he'd just received because—because Jill had climbed over the railing.

What in the hell was she doing?

Jill? He took a step toward her.

She jumped into the water. Just plunged straight into the waves.

Jill!

Chapter Fifteen

The water was colder than she'd expected. Ice-cold. It chilled her limbs, stole her breath and made every stroke that she took painful. Her wet clothes dragged at her, and Jill had to kick out of her shoes. She'd always been a good swimmer, thank goodness, so even the rough waves didn't stop her.

The salt water burned her nose, stung her face, had her coughing as the waves lapped at her face, but she could see the boat. Rising out of the darkness, hidden, because it was so far away from the beach. Anchored and waiting for her, it was at least a twenty-seven-foot sport yacht. She couldn't make out the name on the boat, not in the dark, but she saw the line of letters near the bow. Jill swam to the back of the boat, and her hand curled around the ladder there. She pulled herself up, her breath heaving out of her lungs. She stood there a moment, water pooling down her body and a bright light shone straight into her eyes.

"Hello, Jillian…"

His voice wasn't rasping any longer. Wasn't disguised. She knew his voice. She knew him. But then, Jill had known his identity even before she'd jumped into the water. She'd known when he called her on that beach. When he'd said…

It's your fault she's dead…you did all this. Destroyed the life I had.

Those had actually been words she'd heard before…from Theodore Anderson.

"Hello, Mr. Anderson," Jill said. She kept one hand behind her back. She didn't want him to see that she had the screwdriver tucked into her sleeve. When she'd pulled herself up the ladder, she'd pushed the screwdriver up her sleeve. Easy access. Perfect access.

But first I need to make sure Vanessa is here.

"Jillian West." He didn't take the light off her face. "Looking a bit worse for wear. Guess you didn't get out of that cabin unscathed, after all."

"No, I didn't." But she wasn't talking about the bomb. She was talking about a time long ago. "I came alone, just like you ordered. Now show me Vanessa."

"She's in the cabin below."

He had a gun in one hand. She could see its bulky shape just beyond the light.

"I need to see her," Jill snapped.

He laughed. "You aren't giving orders out here. You're not the big, bad FBI agent out here. You know what you are?" He took a gliding step toward her.

She shivered in the cold air.

"You're my victim," he told her, voice growling. "And tonight, you're going to die."

No, I'm not.

KURT RAN A trembling hand over his face. "My dad used to have an old fishing boat that he'd take out when he was in town. The weekend Christy went missing...the night that Jillian West was taken...he *was* out fishing. I'd seen him loading up his boat. He even told me where he was planning to go...skimming out in the Gulf, maybe heading toward Destin."

Samantha just stared at him. She felt her phone vibrate in her pocket, but she didn't pull it out. Not yet.

"But he came back," Kurt mumbled as he started to pace amid the chaos of the den. "I saw him that morning. He was in and he was... he was so mad. Drinking. I told you, he changed when he drank. He was yelling. Furious. So I went in my room and I stayed away from him."

"Your sister didn't stay away," Samantha said. "You sent her out to him."

Kurt stilled. "I asked him about her. Dad said he never saw Christy that day, that he went back down to his boat. See—it was just a mix-up, that's all. Dad *never* saw Christy."

Her gaze slid toward Blake. His jaw was locked, his eyes glinting.

Her phone vibrated again, reminding her that she'd received a text. "Excuse me a moment." She slipped back a few feet and pulled out her phone. She saw the text—a group text that had been sent to her and Hayden Blake.

A text from Jill.

Come to pier. Perp on boat. Has V.

She took in a long, slow breath. "Kurt, does your father still have that fishing boat?"

"No." He shook his head, but then he pressed his lips together.

"Kurt?" Blake prompted, voice tight.

"He…he has a sports yacht now. Bought it after he got sober. Said it was his present to himself." Kurt licked his lips. "The boat's called *Christy*."

"Thank you for your time," Samantha said. She turned on her heel. Strode for the door.

"That's it?" Kurt yelled after her. Then she heard the fast rush of his footsteps. "No way, lady, you said you'd help me find my dad. You said— Ow! Let me the hell go!"

She whipped around to see Blake standing between her and Kurt. Blake had grabbed the other man's wrist.

"He was lunging for you," Blake said, shaking his head. "A bad mistake." He released Kurt, but his body was tense, as if he were ready to attack again.

Kurt's cheeks had flushed. "I just need to find my dad. Will you help me find him or not?"

Her gaze sharpened on him. "You're afraid of what he'll do, aren't you?"

She saw the answer in the sudden widening of Kurt's eyes.

"I'm afraid, too," she told him, her words nearly a whisper. "But don't worry. We're going to find him. And the *Christy*." She curled her fingers around Blake's shoulder. "Come on. We need to leave. *Now*." They hurried back into the night and she ran for the car. Blake was right on her heels.

"Samantha, slow down!" Blake urged.

They didn't have time to slow down. She yanked open her door.

He grabbed the door and held tight. "Tell me what the hell is going on."

"Jillian found the killer."

"What?"

"I think she's on the *Christy* with him—and Vanessa is there. We have to get out there, now." She shoved his hand off the door. "So come on, let's get moving! Jillian needs us, and I'm not about to let her down."

JILLIAN'S FINGERS CURLED around the screwdriver as she slid it into her palm. "I want you to bring Vanessa out to me."

Theodore didn't move. "It's your fault."

So he liked to keep saying.

"I had it all planned. You were going to be perfect. The new girl in town, the one that didn't fit in. I'd never taken a girl from Hope before, too close to home, if you know what I mean."

He'd been living in that town, for all those years...

"But you were perfect. Like a little bonus gift."

She edged closer to him. He had the gun in his right hand, but he wasn't aiming it at her. Just holding it by his side.

"Then you got away." Anger roughed his voice. The boat rocked in the water. "You weren't supposed to get away. What if you brought the police to me? I tried to be careful, tried to make sure that you didn't see me too clearly but I was afraid..."

"And people who are afraid make terrible

mistakes." She slipped forward. "Is that what Christy was? A mistake?"

"She...she found me in the garage. I had... I had the rope and the drugs I'd used on you. Christy asked me what I was doing. Your story... it had just been on the news. My girl saw it. She stared at me and in her eyes, I knew she realized what I'd done."

Had she, though? Had Christy put the pieces together just based on a rope? Or had this twisted killer before her snapped and taken his own daughter's life?

He lifted his hand—the hand with the gun— and still didn't even seem to notice he held the weapon. He slammed the back of his hand against the side of his head hitting himself hard. *Punishing* himself? "The urge was so strong. I had to kill, but *you* were supposed to be the one. Only you got away. Christy was there. Staring at me. I saw the truth in her eyes... *I saw.* I lunged for her and she screamed." He hit his head again. "Christy screamed. I couldn't let her scream."

And he'd killed his own daughter. But he'd actually felt remorse for her death. *Unlike the others.* "You took her body to the beach..."

"She loved the beach," he whispered. "Just like me. Always loved the water."

"You covered her up. Positioned her." All signs of remorse. Of care.

His hand fell away from his head. "It should have been you."

The gun was pointed at her now. *Great. Now he remembers the weapon.*

"If you'd died, Christy would have been safe. I would never have hurt her."

Like she believed that one. "How many girls have you hurt?"

He didn't speak. She couldn't see his face clearly but was he smiling?

"Hard to remember them all," he admitted. "After Christy, I stopped. Lost so much. Lost *me.* The drinking numbed everything. The days slid by. I let everything go. Then Kurt came back. Made me get clean. Everything started to focus again...and then, as if right on time, you came back. I knew what I had to do. Once I kill you, I can get back the life I had."

Jill shook her head. "That's not going to happen."

He put the light down on the seat near him, and that bright glow stayed locked on Jill. "No one is here to save you."

"*I'm* here to save Vanessa. That was part of the deal, remember? I come here and you let her go."

He advanced toward Jill. "Guess what, *Agent* West? I lied about the deal. I'm planning to kill you both. I told you... *I'm* getting my life back. My life. My power. My control."

Because that was what it had always been about. Control. Dominance. "Guess what?" She threw those words back at him as Jill tightened her grip on that screwdriver. She could have tried to use her gun, but if the water had jammed the weapon, she'd lose her chance to attack. "I lied, too."

His arm jerked and the gun's nozzle pointed down at the deck. "What?"

"I texted Hayden and one of my contacts at the FBI." She used her left hand to point toward the beach. "They're all out there now." Or, if they weren't, they'd be there soon. "They know about you and the boat, and you're not getting away this time. You're going to pay for everything that you've done."

"You damn—" He lifted that gun again.

But Jill was running forward. She lifted up her screwdriver and lunged for him. The gun exploded and she felt the bullet whip past her shoulder, burning into the skin as it grazed her arm.

She drove the screwdriver at him, sinking it into his shoulder. He roared his rage and lifted that gun again.

They were close, her head tipped back as she stared up at his eyes. The monster from the dark. The one who'd haunted her for so long.

She yanked the screwdriver out of him and prepared to hit him again.

He fired. This time, the bullet slammed into her side. She staggered back.

"Jill!" At that wild roar, her head whipped around. Hayden was there, pulling himself up the ladder, water pouring off him. His hands were fisted, the bright light aimed in his direction and clearly showing the rage on his face.

Her feet slipped and she tumbled down, slamming into the back of the seat.

"Just had to follow her again, didn't you?" Theodore snarled. "Always messing things up for me...*always*..."

"Get away from her," Hayden shouted.

But Theodore lifted his gun. "Time to end you, too. Shouldn't have played hero. Not then, not now."

"Stop!" Jill yelled. She'd yanked out the gun from her ankle holster. She pointed it at Theodore. "Drop your weapon, *now*!"

He laughed. "You just swam through the damn Gulf of Mexico. That weapon isn't going to fire. You think I didn't realize you'd have a gun with you? It's useless. *Useless.* But mine isn't."

He was going to shoot Hayden. *Not Hayden. Not Hayden.* "No!" She squeezed the trigger and the damn thing didn't fire. It just clicked. The weapon didn't shoot—

But Theodore's did. His weapon fired even as Hayden slammed into him. The two men staggered at the impact and then—

They fell off the side of the boat, sinking into the waves with a splash.

"Hayden!" She grabbed the light and scrambled to the side, ignoring the pain from her wound.

Had the bullet hit him before they went over? She kept one hand at her side, trying to stop the blood from pumping out and her other hand gripped the light. She swept it over the waves, searching frantically for Hayden. She put her foot on the side of the boat, ready to jump in after him, ready to do anything, risk *anything* for him—

Hayden's head broke the surface.

Her breath left her in a frantic rush.

He swam toward the boat. Strong, powerful strokes. She ran to the back, dropping the light and she grabbed his arm to help pull him on board. Pain knifed through her, surging from her wound, and she bit back a ragged gasp.

Then Hayden was in front. Wet, strong, *alive*. Her pain didn't matter. *He's safe.*

"That bastard shot you." Hayden put his hand on her side. "Baby, I'm so sorry. I'm—"

She kissed him. Fast. Hard. Wild. *Wrong time,*

wrong place. She knew that and didn't care. "You're okay." The words tumbled out, so frantic. "When you went over, I was so scared." More scared than she'd ever been in her life. "You're okay."

"Jill, you're the one who was shot." His fingers tested her wound and he swore. "Too much blood, baby, too much. You need help."

She needed him. And he was there. *Safe.* "He told me not to tell anyone. Said he'd kill Vanessa." *Vanessa.* Jill glanced back at the stairs that led belowdecks. "She's down there. We have to make sure she's—" Her body trembled.

Hayden scooped her in his arms and carried her to the seat behind the wheel. He sat her down with gentle care. "I'll check. You stay here." His gaze scanned the darkness around them. "I don't know where that jerk is. He could be at the bottom of the Gulf, he could be swimming away, or he could be coming back for us."

She grabbed his shirt. "Make sure Vanessa is okay."

He snatched up the radio and called in a quick Mayday, demanding help and, after a fast glance at the screen near the steering wheel, he rattled off their coordinates to the Coast Guard. Then he bent down and kissed her once more.

Hayden. Alive. We're both safe.

He picked up the gun that had fallen when he

and Theodore had gone over the side of the boat. "If you see him—"

Jill's fingers curled around the gun. "Don't worry. I won't hesitate. He's destroyed enough lives."

Hayden nodded. Then he turned and rushed toward the stairs.

Jill gripped the gun and she stared into the darkness around the boat. Her heartbeat seemed to thunder in her ears. Her side burned, the blood soaking her shirt and making it cling to her skin. The moments ticked by. The boat bobbed, pulling against its anchor.

"She's all right." Hayden appeared, holding a girl tightly in his arms. "She's okay, Jill. You got to her in time."

He put Vanessa down on the deck, and he started yanking at the ropes that still bound her hands. Jill saw that a gag had been pulled away from the girl's mouth.

Tears stung Jill's eyes. *Safe.*

"I—I want to go home," Vanessa rasped.

"You will," Jill promised her. "We're going to take you home. Everything is going to be okay." *She's alive. We found her alive.*

But the man who'd taken her... Jill's gaze dipped to the waves...

Where are you, Theodore Anderson? Where did you go?

THE DOCK BLAZED with lights. Deputies, EMTs, hell, half of the town seemed to be there when they finally made it to shore.

Jill was immediately put on a stretcher. Hayden saw an EMT start to cut away the bloody shirt that clung to Jill's side. He stepped forward—

"Stay with Vanessa!" Jill cried out, her frantic gaze locking with his. "Make sure she's okay—her family—"

He had his arm around Vanessa's shoulder. She was trembling against him. Shaking. He'd checked her out on the boat and she seemed unharmed, thank Christ.

Theodore Anderson. Theodore damn Anderson. The killer had been right there, all along.

Samantha Dark pushed through the crowd and rushed to Jill's side. "What happened?"

A tall, dark-haired man was right behind her. His gaze swept the crowd, then locked on Hayden.

FBI. Hell, that truth pretty much rolled off that guy. Hayden pegged him with one glance.

"Come on, Vanessa," Hayden said softly. "We'll get you checked out." He motioned toward another EMT and the fellow hurried toward them. He caught sight of Finn, and Hayden jerked his hand at the deputy. Finn shot through the assembled group. "*Stay* with her, got me? In the ambulance, every single minute." Because he was afraid.

Hayden's gaze cut to the water.

The waves were rougher, hitting the dock harder. The boats bobbed in the water.

When they'd gone over the side of the boat, Hayden had heard a distinct *thunk*. They'd been fighting as they fell, and Theodore's head had hit the side of the boat. They'd gone into the water and the waves had ripped them apart.

Hayden had been frantic to get back on the boat, to get back to Jill.

He hadn't searched for Theodore. And the man hadn't come up.

Was he dead?

Or had the bastard gotten away?

"Vanessa!" The scream cut through the crowd. High, desperate. Afraid.

A mother's scream.

Hayden motioned to the deputies, and they immediately cleared a path for Carol Wells so that she could get to her daughter. When Carol appeared, tears were streaming down her cheeks. Her face was stark white and the terror in her eyes made his chest ache.

"She's okay," he said quietly. His hand patted her shoulder and he pushed Carol toward Vanessa as she sat on the edge of a nearby gurney. "She's safe."

Carol stumbled toward her daughter. "I'm so sorry, Vanessa," Carol sobbed. "I'm so sorry, I'm so sorry…"

"Mom." Vanessa was crying, too. She lifted her arms. "Mom!"

They hugged tight. Hayden stared at them a moment. Their family wasn't perfect. No family was. But Vanessa was safe. Alive. They could deal with the problems that came their way. They had a chance now.

A chance that Theodore wouldn't take away from them.

He grabbed Finn's arm. "You stay with them, every minute, got it?" Hayden ordered again, because fear gnawed at him. Theodore Anderson didn't let his victims go easily.

"I won't let you down," Finn promised.

Hayden slipped away from him. Jill was being loaded into the back of an ambulance. She was fighting the EMT—why the hell was the woman doing that? "Jill!" He ran to her.

"I need to stay here!" Jill snapped to the EMT. "He's still out there—I have to make sure they find him—I can't go!"

"Hell, yes, you can," Hayden growled.

Samantha and the dark-haired man with her were huddled near the back of the ambulance. At his words, they both looked his way.

So did Jill.

But when she stared at him, Hayden saw her gaze soften.

She still looks at me the same way. Only Jill had ever looked at him like that. With eyes wide with hope and...love. It was still there. He hadn't destroyed it years ago, as he'd feared.

It was still there.

"You need to get to a hospital," he said, and he climbed right into the back of the ambulance with her. "Baby, you need stitches and you lost a whole lot of blood. You have to let the EMTs and the docs take care of you."

She grabbed his hand and held tight. "But Theodore's still out there."

"I'll keep the search going." He brought her hand to his lips. Kissed her. For an instant, his eyes closed and he remembered swimming desperately to that boat, grabbing the ladder, seeing her—and hearing the boom of the gun. "Thought I lost you." The terror was still inside him, twisting at his gut, hollowing his insides. "You've got to stop doing this to me."

His eyes opened.

Jill was staring at him the same way—

"God, I love you so much, Jill," he told her.

Her lips parted.

"You're giving me that chance we talked about," he said quickly. "You're going to get stitched up, you're going to heal, and we'll start fresh."

But... Jill shook her head.

That twisting inside of him turned into ice-cold fear. "What?"

"Don't need to start fresh..." She wet her lips. "Still...love you."

He leaned over.

"Uh, excuse me, Sheriff," the EMT began.

Hayden's hands were careful as they brushed Jill's hair away from her cheek. "I've loved you since I was fifteen years old. You've always been my world." He needed her to understand this. "I will *never* stop loving you." Just as he'd never stop fighting for her, for them.

He pressed a kiss to her lips. Gentle. Tender. "You saved her, Jill. You brought Vanessa home."

Her lips curved into a faint smile.

"And you saved me." She always had. "So do me a damn favor, okay?" Now his voice was rough. "Go to the hospital because I need you okay. You *have* to be okay." She was everything to him. And just seeing her in pain ripped him apart.

Jill nodded.

His breath expelled in a rush.

"Finish the search," Jill ordered quickly. "Stay

here, Hayden. Make sure the crews look everywhere."

"Yes, ma'am." He squeezed her fingers once more, and then he slid from the back of the ambulance. His gaze jerked to Samantha. "Will you—"

She was already climbing into the vehicle. "Don't worry. I'll stay with her the whole time. I'll make sure she's a good patient and that she's safe."

Hell, yes.

That twisting inside eased as he backed away and the ambulance roared from the scene with a squeal of its sirens.

When she was clear, when Jill was gone, a long sigh eased from him.

"Must've been hard…"

Hayden glanced at the guy he'd pegged as an FBI agent.

The man pulled out his ID and flashed it at him. "Blake Gamble. I'm Samantha's new partner. Came down to assist her and Jillian. Though it looks like I was late to most of the party."

"Party's not over," Hayden denied grimly. "Theodore Anderson is still out there." But he'd just caught sight of a familiar face in the crowd. A face that was staring at the scene in shocked horror.

Kurt Anderson's face.

"I can't imagine what it was like," Blake murmured. "Swimming out there, knowing the woman you loved was in danger."

Hayden pulled his gaze off Kurt. *Hard* didn't even begin to describe what it had been like. Try *freaking nightmare.*

"Tell me how I can help," Blake said. "What can I do?"

"Get on a boat." Because search crews were mounting already. The Coast Guard was out, and Hayden was about to hit the water, too. "Let's go find the bastard." He wouldn't be satisfied, not until they'd locked Theodore Anderson in jail.

Or they'd pulled his lifeless body from the water.

Chapter Sixteen

Two weeks later...

The waves pounded against the beach. The sky was dark, clouds covering the stars, so Jill couldn't see the whitecaps as they hit the shore. She stood on the deck of her cabin, her heart beating slowly, her gaze on the darkness.

Theodore Anderson hadn't been found. He hadn't come home. His body hadn't washed ashore.

Had he died out there? And his body had been pulled out to sea?

Or had he slipped away? Was he already planning another attack? Another abduction?

Warm hands slid down her arms, and she felt Hayden's strong body press to her back. "I still have patrols searching the town."

She knew he did. But the media circus that had hit the area when news broke about Theodore Anderson—that madness had died away. Thankfully. Life was starting to get back to normal for everyone in Hope.

Well…for most people.

Normal would be a long time coming for Vanessa. Her brother had returned to town, and Jill knew that Porter was staying close to his sister. Protecting her.

And as for Kurt…he'd already put his house up for sale. When she'd talked to him after getting out of the hospital, he'd seemed to be a broken shell of himself.

"Do you think he's dead?" Jill asked. She turned in Hayden's arms, putting her back against the wooden balcony railing.

His gaze lifted and focused over her shoulder, on the darkness that was behind her. "I won't believe he's dead, not until I see a body. Until then, he's a threat. One that I won't ever forget."

That was how she felt, too. Like she just couldn't let go. "I looked over my shoulder for half of my life, always thinking the monster from the dark was out there." And he had been. "Now the monster has a face."

"He *won't* take you again." Fierce determination thickened his voice.

"No." She was certain of this, too. Because she wasn't a victim, not anymore. "He won't." Theodore Anderson was prey. Hunted by local authorities, by the FBI. His face had been on every newscast in the country. He was a wanted man.

He would be found.

"Jill, I have something to ask you." Hayden backed away from her. Exhaled slowly. He seemed…nervous. Odd, for Hayden. "I know that your job base is in Atlanta. Your team wants you back up there."

Yes, they did. But she'd been given extra leave in spite of…well, *everything*.

"Atlanta, Hope, wherever you want to be… I'd like to be with you." He bent down before her.

OhmyGod… He was on one knee. Hayden pulled a small, black box from his pocket. He opened it, and the ring sparkled in the dark. "I've loved you since I met you. Time just made that feeling even stronger. I want to spend my life with you. I want *you*, Jill. Always, you." And, once more, he gave a quick, nervous exhale. "Will you marry me?"

She stared at the ring, and then she looked at what really mattered… Hayden. Hayden's eyes. Her Hayden. And she smiled at him. "Yes."

He surged up to his feet. He put the ring on her finger and then he was kissing her. Wildly. Hotly. Happily.

There was so much emotion in his touch. So much joy. Jill felt that same joy. She wasn't going to let fear hold her back any longer. Yes, there were bad things in this world. So many bad things...

But there were good things, too. Kisses, smiles, love...hope.

Girls who were reunited with their families. People who fought to protect victims. People who cared.

The good beat the bad.

It won.

She curled her arms around Hayden's neck. He picked her up and carried her inside, stopping just long enough to lock the sliding glass door. Then he was walking through the cabin and taking her to the bedroom. He put her on the bed, his touch so very careful.

She smiled at him. "I'm not going to break."

"I know, baby. You proved that long ago." He tossed his shirt into the corner. Kicked off his shoes and socks and slid onto the edge of the bed. "But you're still healing and—"

She curled her fingers around his shoulder. "I'm all healed, Hayden. And I want you." Every bit of him. She kissed him, then bit his lower lip, a sexy tease that she knew he loved.

She toed out of her shoes and sent them flying. Then Hayden's hand was at the zipper of her jeans. The faint hiss seemed loud in the quiet room. He pushed down the jeans, shoved down her underwear, but when his fingers slid between her legs…he was so gentle.

Careful.

I told him I wouldn't break.

He stroked her, arousing her desire to a fever pitch, making her hips jerk against him. She still had on her shirt and her tight nipples thrust forward. "Hayden!"

His hand slid away from her. He jerked off her shirt, his touch a bit rougher now, but he didn't so much as brush her healing wound. The bullet wound that would always remind her of Theodore.

Hayden unhooked her bra. He put his mouth on her breast and she choked out his name as heated sensation poured through her. She loved Hayden's touch. Loved his mouth. Loved the way he made her feel.

But she hated it when the man made her wait.

Jill's fingers slid between their bodies. She found his heavy length—thick, hot, fully aroused. She pumped him, enjoying the feel of him in her hands. Then she pushed the head of his arousal between her legs. She needed this moment. She needed him. "Hayden." His name was a demand.

He kissed her neck, right over her pulse, in that spot that drove her crazy.

Then he thrust into her. For an instant, she

could have sworn that time froze. Everything was perfect for her—love, need, desire…

Hayden.

Then he withdrew, only to drive deep into her once more. The bed squeaked beneath him. Her legs wrapped around his hips. Deeper, harder, he pistoned his hips against her. And Jill couldn't hold back her release. Her nails sank into his back and she called out his name as the pleasure broke over her.

Hayden was with her. He sank into her core once more, and then he stiffened. He whispered her name as he came, a long shudder driving over him, and he held her tight. So tight.

As if he'd never let go. That was good, so good, because Jill never intended to let him go, either.

In the aftermath, Hayden pulled her close. Their fingers twined together. The diamond ring shined in the night.

And Jill closed her eyes.

IT WAS THE squeak that woke her later. The squeak that came from the sliding glass door that led out to her balcony. Her eyes flew open and she sucked in a quick breath.

"It's okay," Hayden whispered. His fingers squeezed hers.

But…it wasn't okay. Someone was breaking into her cabin.

"We were waiting for this," Hayden said. His hand slipped from hers. He opened the nightstand drawer and took out two guns.

Because, yes, they had known that if Theodore Anderson lived, he might try to attack again. That was the reason Jill had stayed in the same cabin on the beach. Why she'd been sure to go out on the deck every evening.

Bait.

She hadn't wanted Theodore to go after Vanessa. *I wanted him to come after me.*

She slid on a T-shirt and her shorts as Hayden jerked on his jeans. Then, armed, they both moved soundlessly toward her bedroom door.

She heard the groan from the outer room. Their intruder was near the TV. Hadn't he learned from last time? No, obviously not, he was making all of the same mistakes.

But I'm not.

She released a slow breath, and then Jill nodded toward Hayden. *Ready.* She mouthed the word at him.

He yanked open the door.

"Freeze!" Jill yelled.

Hayden hit the light. Illumination flooded onto Theodore Anderson as he stood in the middle of her den. Heavy stubble covered his jaw and in his hand, he held a long, glinting knife.

A knife wouldn't do much good against two guns. "You're under arrest," Jill said.

He screamed at her and he lifted his hand and charged right toward her. In that split second, she understood that he'd rather die than go to jail. For a man like him, prison would be a living hell. The girls he'd killed…his own daughter…

The other inmates would make him pay, every single day—and night.

Theodore Anderson wanted to die. He wanted to be taken out.

But on that boat, he'd boasted about other victims. Victims that the authorities hadn't identified. Those families deserved closure.

"Stop!" Jill yelled. She fired, just as Hayden fired.

Her bullet hit Theodore in the leg. Hayden's bullet slammed into the guy's shoulder. Theodore fell to the floor, injured, but not dead. *It won't be that easy for you.*

"No!" The anguished bellow had Jill's head jerking up and swinging to the left—toward her open screen door. Kurt Anderson stood there, his eyes wild, glittering. "You have to kill him! *You have to kill him!*"

And Kurt pulled out a gun.

"Was watching the house…waiting…knew

he'd come back…" Kurt's words were slurred. *Drunk. Pain filled.* "H-he hated you so much… knew he'd come back…have to stop him." His weapon pointed at his father.

Hayden had kicked Theodore's knife away from the injured man. "He is stopped, Kurt. Your father is *done*. He's going to prison, and he won't hurt anyone again."

The gun trembled in Kurt's hand. "Prison… won't bring Christy back."

Jill eased forward. "Killing him won't do that, either."

But Kurt smiled. "Killing him…will make me feel a whole lot better."

"Is that what Christy would have wanted?" Jill asked him, desperate. *I didn't think about Kurt…all the pain he felt… I should have realized he wouldn't let his father go.*

"Don't know what Christy wants," Kurt's breath heaved out. "She's dead. Can't ask her. He *took* her…and lied…lied for so long." He shook his head. She saw the tear tracks on his cheeks. "No more. No *more!*"

Kurt was going to fire. Jill knew it. She didn't want to shoot him but—

Hayden launched his body at Kurt's, tackling the other man. They fell against the couch. The bullet fired, but it went wild, blasting into the TV and shattering the screen.

"You aren't like him," Hayden said as he held the other man down. "You're stronger. *You aren't like him. We don't have to be like our fathers.*"

Kurt started crying—choking out hard sobs— as all of the fight went out of him. Hayden rose to his feet, tucking the gun he'd taken from Kurt into the back of his jeans and— "Jill!" Hayden roared her name, his eyes flaring wide.

She'd thought Theodore was beaten. Thought he was out. But at Hayden's frantic yell, her gaze flew to the fallen man.

Theodore had pulled a switchblade from his boot. He was struggling to get to her.

No, he's still trying to control me. "You don't have the control any longer." She kicked the backup knife out of his hand. "Jail is waiting for you. Punishment is waiting. There's no easy out."

At her words, something seemed to break in him. He screamed at her and staggered to his feet. He came at her with his fists clenched, his eyes bulging—

Hayden stepped in front of her before she could attack. "Been waiting years for this…" He drove his fist into Theodore's face. One punch. Another. Again and again and the older man stumbled back. Hayden was relentless, hitting, striking out with powerful blows and Theodore fell back against the wall. "You never should have taken her," Hayden's deep voice rumbled with his rage. "Never—"

Jill caught his hand before he could strike again. Theodore's eyes had rolled back into his head. The man was out cold, slumped on the floor. "Hayden," Jill said his name softly.

He looked at her. She saw the rage and pain in his eyes…and the fear.

But beneath it all, Jill saw his love for her.

"We're safe." She smiled at him. "And it's over." The nightmare that had started so long ago was over. Theodore wasn't getting away. He wouldn't take anyone else. There would be no more death left in his wake.

The end had come for the nightmare that had haunted them all for so long.

HAYDEN STOOD AT the end of the pier. His gaze was on the water below him, deep blue water.

He heard the soft pad of footsteps and glanced back to see Jill walking toward him. Beautiful Jill. Her red hair gleamed in the setting sun.

When she reached his side, Jill said, "Samantha is working on getting the names of his other victims. I… I asked her to handle the interrogation because I knew he'd just try to play me. It's too personal with him. With us." Her gaze slid toward the water. "But Samantha is the damn best there is at getting killers to talk. She'll find the truth for us. I know it."

Her hand curled over the railing. The diamond ring he'd given to her shined. He put his hand on top of hers. Squeezed.

Same pier. Same girl.

New life.

"I love you, Jill," he told her, aware that his voice had thickened. They'd had a plan in place, anticipating that Theodore might strike but when the guy had gone for her again, when he'd leaped at Jill, something had snapped inside of Hayden. He'd attacked. Fought back with the wild fury of the boy he'd been…and of the man who couldn't stand for another to ever threaten the woman he loved.

She leaned closer and pressed a kiss to his cheek. Surprised, he looked at her.

She was smiling. Such a beautiful, warm smile. No shadows were in her eyes. Just peace. Just…

Hope.

"I know," Jill told him softly. "And I love you, too. You're my partner, my lover…and my very best friend."

Her friend.

"You always have been," she said.

Just as she had been his…everything.

"Forever, Hayden?"

He pulled her into his arms and held her tight. "Hell, yes, baby. Hell, yes." As the waves pounded beneath him, Hayden kissed her.

* * * * *

LARGER-PRINT BOOKS!

GET 2 FREE LARGER-PRINT NOVELS PLUS
2 FREE GIFTS!

HARLEQUIN®

Romance

From the Heart, For the Heart

HRLP15

LARGER-PRINT BOOKS!
GET 2 FREE LARGER-PRINT NOVELS PLUS
2 FREE GIFTS!

HARLEQUIN

super romance

More Story...More Romance

YES! Please send me 2 FREE LARGER-PRINT Harlequin® Superromance® novels and my 2 FREE gifts (gifts are worth about $10). After receiving them, if I don't wish to receive any more books, I can return the shipping statement marked "cancel." If I don't cancel, I will receive 4 brand-new novels every month and be billed just $5.94 per book in the U.S. or $6.24 per book in Canada. That's a savings of at least 12% off the cover price! It's quite a bargain! Shipping and handling is just 50¢ per book in the U.S. or 75¢ per book in Canada.* I understand that accepting the 2 free books and gifts places me under no obligation to buy anything. I can always return a shipment and cancel at any time. Even if I never buy another book, the two free books and gifts are mine to keep forever.

132/332 HDN GHVC

Name _____ (PLEASE PRINT)

Address _____ Apt. #

City _____ State/Prov. _____ Zip/Postal Code

Signature (if under 18, a parent or guardian must sign)

Mail to the **Reader Service:**
IN U.S.A.: P.O. Box 1867, Buffalo, NY 14240-1867
IN CANADA: P.O. Box 609, Fort Erie, Ontario L2A 5X3

Want to try two free books from another line?
Call 1-800-873-8635 today or visit www.ReaderService.com.

* Terms and prices subject to change without notice. Prices do not include applicable taxes. Sales tax applicable in N.Y. Canadian residents will be charged applicable taxes. Offer not valid in Quebec. This offer is limited to one order per household. Not valid for current subscribers to Harlequin Superromance Larger-Print books. All orders subject to credit approval. Credit or debit balances in a customer's account(s) may be offset by any other outstanding balance owed by or to the customer. Please allow 4 to 6 weeks for delivery. Offer available while quantities last.

Your Privacy—The Reader Service is committed to protecting your privacy. Our Privacy Policy is available online at www.ReaderService.com or upon request from the Reader Service.

We make a portion of our mailing list available to reputable third parties that offer products we believe may interest you. If you prefer that we not exchange your name with third parties, or if you wish to clarify or modify your communication preferences, please visit us at www.ReaderService.com/consumerchoice or write to us at Reader Service Preference Service, P.O. Box 9062, Buffalo, NY 14240-9062. Include your complete name and address.

HSRLP15

WESTERN WP PROMISES

YES! Please send me **The Western Promises Collection** in Larger Print. This collection begins with 3 FREE books and 2 FREE gifts (gifts valued at approx. $14.00 retail) in the first shipment, along with the other first 4 books from the collection! If I do not cancel, I will receive 8 monthly shipments until I have the entire 51-book Western Promises collection. I will receive 2 or 3 FREE books in each shipment and I will pay just $4.99 US/ $5.89 CDN for each of the other four books in each shipment, plus $2.99 for shipping and handling per shipment. *If I decide to keep the entire collection, I'll have paid for only 32 books, because 19 books are FREE! I understand that accepting the 3 free books and gifts places me under no obligation to buy anything. I can always return a shipment and cancel at any time. My free books and gifts are mine to keep no matter what I decide.

272 HCN 3070 472 HCN 3070

Name   (PLEASE PRINT)

Address   Apt. #

City   State/Prov.   Zip/Postal Code

Signature (if under 18, a parent or guardian must sign)

Mail to the **Reader Service:**
IN U.S.A.: P.O. Box 1867, Buffalo, NY 14240-1867 .
IN CANADA: P.O. Box 609, Fort Erie, Ontario L2A 5X3

* Terms and prices subject to change without notice. Prices do not include applicable taxes. Sales tax applicable in N.Y. Canadian residents will be charged applicable taxes. This offer is limited to one order per household. All orders subject to approval. Credit or debit balances in a customer's account(s) may be offset by any other outstanding balance owed by or to the customer. Please allow 4 to 6 weeks for delivery. Offer available while quantities last. Offer not available to Quebec residents.

Your Privacy—The Reader Service is committed to protecting your privacy. Our Privacy Policy is available online at www.ReaderService.com or upon request from the Reader Service.

We make a portion of our mailing list available to reputable third parties that offer products we believe may interest you. If you prefer that we not exchange your name with third parties, or if you wish to clarify or modify your communication preferences, please visit us at www.ReaderService.com/consumerschoice or write to us at Reader Service Preference Service, P.O. Box 9062, Buffalo, NY 14240-9062. Include your complete name and address.

WPBPA16R